A JESTER'S HEART

Trials of a Jester's Fate

Nicholas Cairo Valdes

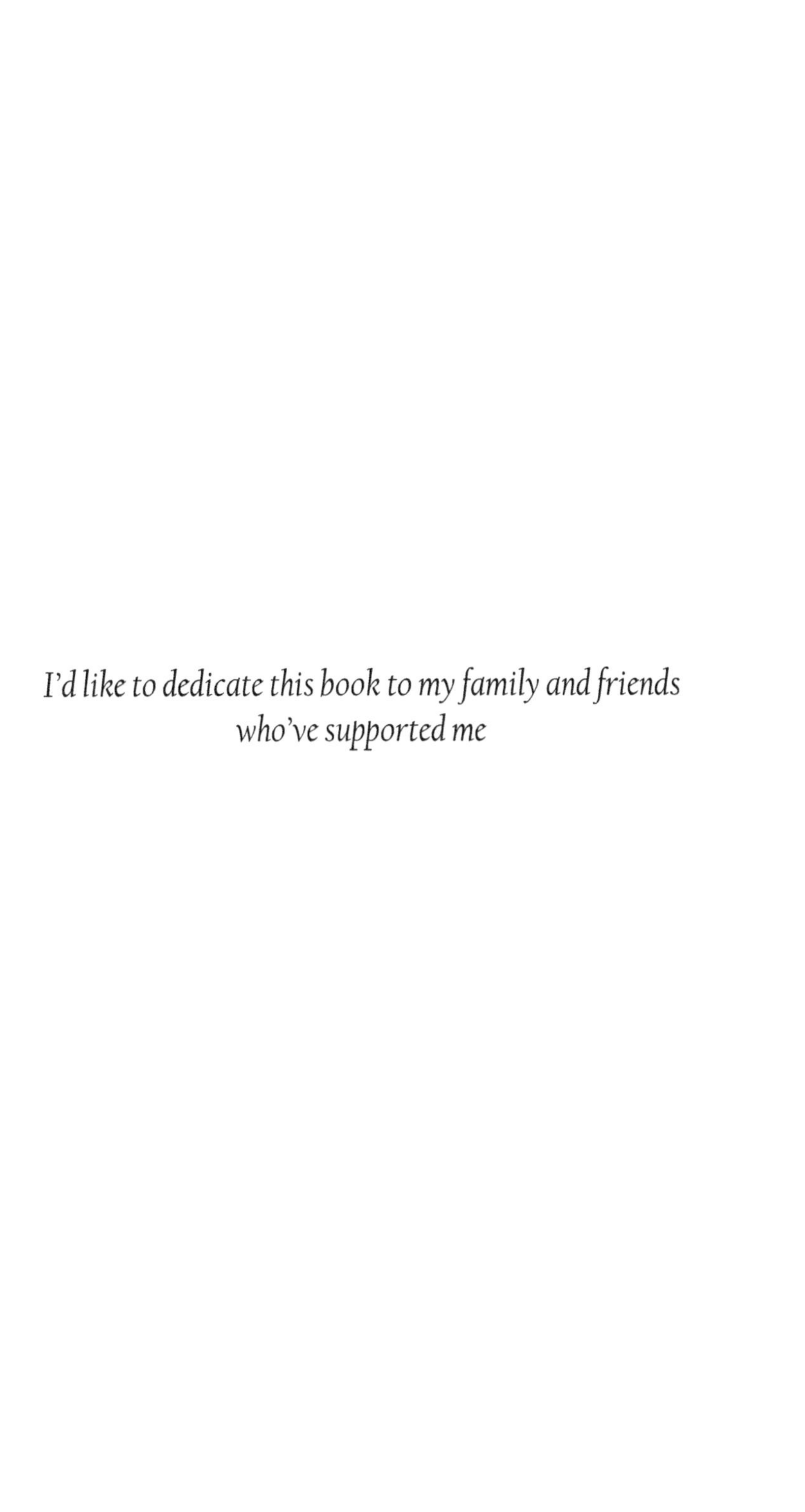

I'd like to dedicate this book to my family and friends who've supported me

TABLE OF CONTENTS

Chapter One: One man's Dream 1

Chapter Two: The Fool's Beginning 4

Chapter Three: The Bond Forged in Twilight.............. 18

Chapter Four: A Brotherhood Formed...........................34

Chapter Five: The Warrior and The Jester 46

Chapter Six: Siege of Castle Jezik 60

Chapter Seven: An audience with the King..................68

Chapter Eight: Contest of Fools 73

Chapter Nine: No comedy without tragedy 94

Chapter Ten: Taken 123

Chapter Eleven: Medicine and tears........................ 132

Chapter Twelve: The Hanged Jester........................149

Chapter Thirteen: Epilogue 164

CHAPTER ONE:
One man's Dream

What is a jester? That was the question whispered by a young man as he prepared to ascend the platform where he would meet his fate. His crime? You might wonder. It was as simple as it was cruel: he dared to love the wrong people. As he stood there, pondering where his life had gone astray, his once-vibrant attire hung in dirty, tattered shreds, and his cherished mask lay shattered on the ground.

The executioner approached the young man, securing the noose around his neck and guiding him to the center of the platform, where a trapdoor awaited. Moments later, a man clad in extravagant attire ascended the stage, addressing both the condemned and the gathered crowd—a motley assembly of peasants, nobles, performers, cutthroats, and even the Royal Family. The King wore a sorrowful expression, as though he were about to lose a beloved child. In stark contrast, the Queen's face twisted into a gruesome grin, relishing the scene before her.

Their two children, unable to bear the sight, averted their eyes, while the prince, in particular, seemed deeply troubled. The man in extravagant attire finally raised his voice, clear and commanding. "Today, we are gathered to execute the royal jester for a series of crimes." The young jester swallowed hard, feeling the weight of the hatred in those words. What had he done to deserve such scorn? "His crimes," the man continued, "include one count of debauchery, numerous acts of thievery, and, most grievously, repeated offenses of making the Queen look like a fool."

Despite the noose tightening around his fate, the jester couldn't help but smile, pride flickering in his eyes—making the Queen look foolish was, after all, his finest work. "'One count of murder,'" the man announced sternly. The jester coughed before interjecting, "Actually, it was more of an attempted humiliation that... well, turned into murder."

The King burst into hearty laughter, just as he always did when the jester spoke. But his amusement was swiftly silenced by the Queen's icy glare, sharp enough to pierce armor.

"Right, as you say, you little rat dung," the man retorted, his voice laced with venom.

The jester, unfazed, grinned mischievously. "Actually, it'd be rat droppings—since dung is more of a cow thing. Funny, I thought you'd know, considering you smell like it." The man's face flushed a deep crimson, his fury barely contained. "Laugh whilst thou canst and make all the jests thy heart desires, for soon thou shalt laugh no more," the man sneered, his grim smile widening as he watched the jester's grin fade at last. "Hast thou any final words?". The jester gave a nod. "Aye," he replied, falling silent for a moment as he gathered his thoughts. Finally, he spoke, addressing the crowd.

"What is a jester?" he asked, his voice carrying across the gathered masses. "It is a question I've pondered countless times—in every place I've traveled, with every person I've met."

For once, his playful demeanor gave way to solemnity. "Every answer is different, but one has stayed with me. That answer will remain with me always, just as every connection I've made in my life does—the good ones and the bad."

The man in extravagant attire, unmoved by the jester's words, coldly signaled for the executioner to proceed. Without hesitation, the executioner obeyed.

The noose tightened, stealing the jester's breath. He felt his neck strain and snap as his life began to slip away. In his final moments, scenes of his past flooded his mind, all leading back to one man's dream.

CHAPTER TWO:
The Fool's Beginning

Winter was a cruel season in the humble village of Crovina, nestled on the outskirts of the kingdom of Faldera. The village was small and poor, its meager crops yielding little even in the best of times, and in winter, the hardship grew unbearable. On the edge of the village stood a modest cottage, home to a family of three: Grigori, a hardworking farmer; his five-year-old daughter, Wina—whom he lovingly called Vina; and his wife, Yenn, heavy with child.

Grigori toiled endlessly to provide for his family, for his modest crops brought little profit. Beyond farming, he took on the roles of carpenter, building homes and crafting furniture for the villagers, and even served as the commander of the village guards. His tireless efforts earned him great respect among the people of Crovina.

When he learned his wife was expecting another child, Grigori redoubled his efforts, determined to ensure his family's survival. Though his constant labor often made him seem distant, his love for his family was unwavering. During this harsh winter, Yenn gave birth to a healthy baby boy.

From the moment the baby boy was born, his radiant smile and infectious laughter captivated his family. Yenn adored his cheerful nature and named him Isaak, inspired by the joy his laughter brought.

Years passed, and on Isaak's fifth birthday, he shared his dream with his family: he wished to become a jester, spreading joy and laughter to those who had none. Grigori, though deeply loving his son, could not hide his disappointment. He had hoped Isaak would follow in his footsteps, becoming a farmer to help provide for the family, rather than pursuing the life of a clown.

Yenn, however, saw things differently. She believed Isaak's dream was as fitting as it was beautiful, and she gave him her wholehearted support. His sister agreed, delighting in the idea of her brother bringing joy to the world.

Despite pursuing his dream, Isaak could still feel the weight of his father's disappointment. To ease this, he devoted himself to helping Grigori with the farm, and carpentry, and even joined the village guard. He absorbed all the wisdom his family and the guards could offer, eager to prove himself worthy in his father's eyes.

One figure stood out among his mentors: an old man named Henry, who had once traveled the world in his youth. Isaak was captivated by the elder's tales and would often approach him with wide-eyed excitement, saying, "Sirrah Henry, I beg of thee, tell me more of thy adventures!"

Isaak would often say this while balancing on one leg and giving Henry an exaggerated look of pleading, complete with wide, puppy-like eyes—a gesture that never failed to make the old man laugh.

"Well, Isaak," Henry would chuckle, "give me a good joke, and I'll tell thee a tale. Deal?"

Without hesitation, Isaak would agree, determined to rise to the challenge. Each day, he crafted a new joke just for Henry, whether it was a clever pun or an elaborate, comedic story. Their exchanges became a cherished ritual, blending laughter and storytelling into moments Isaak treasured.

To Isaak, Henry was his first true friend—a bond he cherished as though it were the most precious treasure in the kingdom. He deeply respected the old man and eagerly absorbed his tales of daring adventures and perilous escapades. One story in particular stood out: the time Henry, while poisoned, managed to defeat fifty bandits to obtain the cure.

In his spare moments, when not working, Isaak turned his focus to crafting his dream. He began sewing his own jester's outfit, using his favorite colors—royal purple and passionate red. To complete the ensemble, he carved a wooden mask, simple yet striking: a blank face with eyeholes and a painted grin. Isaak believed a mask with a permanent smile was perfect—no matter his mood, it would allow him to wear a smile, even on the darkest days.

Isaak would carry his wooden box to the center of the village, setting it down in a spot where everyone could see. Climbing atop it, he would cup his hands around his mouth and call out with dramatic flair, "Sirrahs and Madams of all ages, I beseech thee, gather 'round and feast thine eyes upon a spectacle most wondrous!"

His voice rang through the village square, drawing the attention of curious peasants, bustling merchants, and wide-eyed children. Even the village guards paused their patrols to see what the young jester-in-training had in store. Isaak would wave his arms theatrically, adding a flourish to his words as he continued. "Prepare yourselves for a performance the likes of which this humble village hath never seen!"

The anticipation of the crowd grew, murmurs of excitement spreading among them. Isaak basked in their attention, his heart swelling with pride and nerves. This was his stage, and here, he could bring joy and laughter to the people, just as he dreamed.

Isaak would leap into action, dazzling the crowd with flips, handstands, and a series of nimble acrobatic feats. His movements were smooth and confident, each trick earning gasps of amazement and cheers from the onlookers.

As he moved, he kept the crowd entertained with a steady stream of jokes. "And then," he said, pausing for dramatic effect, "the farmer searched high and low for his missing cow—only to find it lying in his bed! The cow looked up and said, 'What is it, husband of mine? 'Twas cold outside!'"

The crowd erupted into laughter, their voices filling the square with joy. Isaak grinned beneath his painted mask, energized by their delight. For a moment, he felt unstoppable, as though he truly could share laughter with anyone who needed it. His tricks and humor worked in perfect harmony, and the village square became a stage for his heart's desire.

Isaak, brimming with joy at the crowd's enthusiasm, decided to end his performance with a special treat for the village children. With a flourish, he reached into the air and, using deft sleight of hand, revealed three eggs in his right hand. Then, with a dramatic spin, he produced three small bottles of paint and three tiny brushes on his left.

Stepping closer to the children, he knelt slightly to meet their eager eyes. "Come hither, young ones!" he said with a playful grin. "I have a task for thee! Each of you shall take an egg and paint upon it your finest, most cheerful smiling faces—not once, but thrice!"

He handed the items to the children, their eyes wide with wonder as they took the eggs and paints. "Once thou art finished," Isaak continued, "return them to me, and thou shalt see what magic awaits!"

The children giggled with excitement, eagerly setting to work as Isaak stood back, watching their enthusiasm with a satisfied smile. He had brought them joy, and that was all he ever wanted.

The children, thrilled by the task, eagerly painted their silliest faces upon the eggs, their imaginations running wild with each stroke of the brush. Isaak watched with delight, his heart swelling with joy at their creativity. Once they had finished, he grinned and began to juggle the eggs, tossing them high into the air with practiced skill.

As he juggled, he spun a whimsical tale for the crowd. "Once upon a time," he began, "there was a mighty dragon, a brave prince, and a jester with a knack for getting into trouble. The jester, by accident, saved the prince from the dragon, not with sword or shield, but with nothing more than his wits and a well-timed pratfall!"

With each toss of the eggs, Isaak's story grew livelier and more exaggerated, making the children giggle and the adult's chuckle. Then, with a wink, he performed another trick. Using his sleight of hand, he made the eggs vanish from mid-air, only to have them reappear in three of the children's pockets.

The crowd erupted in laughter and applause, their cheers ringing through the village square. Isaak stood there, grinning beneath his painted mask, reveling in the joy he had created. The sound of their laughter was music to his ears, and for that moment, he knew he had brought something truly magical to the world.

For most of the day, Isaak felt as though he were soaring on a high, he never thought he could come down from. The joy of his performance, the laughter of the crowd, and the thrill of his magic lingered in his heart. With a sweeping bow, he thanked his audience profusely, his voice filled with gratitude. With a final flip, he leapt from the town center, eager to share his success.

He raced home, his steps light with excitement. Upon entering, he spotted his small, adopted pig, Lawrance, resting comfortably by the hearth. Isaak couldn't bring himself to sell the little creature, having grown so fond of him.

"Lawrance, my faithful friend," he exclaimed, bending down to pet the pig's soft head. "I had the most amazing day!"

The pig gave a simple response, a cheerful oink, as if in agreement with Isaak's exuberance. Isaak smiled warmly, feeling the weight of the day's happiness fill him once more, knowing that, no matter what, his loyal companion would always be there to share in his joy.

Isaak hurried to his mother's room, his heart heavy with both excitement and concern. Inside, he found her lying in bed, her face pale and her body weakened by an illness that no healer had been able to cure. He knelt beside her, his voice filled with tenderness as he asked, "Mama, how fare thee? Do you feel any better?"

His eyes searched her face for a glimmer of hope, but the sorrow in her eyes only deepened his worry. Despite the joy of the day, a shadow of dread lingered in Isaak's heart, knowing his mother's condition was growing worse.

"My dear Isaak, I am fine," his mother said with a gentle smile, though her voice was soft and frail. "I feel fine. But thou, my precious one, art glowing with joy, just as thou didst when thou were but a small babe. What hath brought thee such elation?"

Isaak's face lit up at her words, and he eagerly began recounting his day. He spoke of the crowd's laughter, the children's delight, and his triumphant performance in the town square. As he told his tale, he couldn't resist recreating a few of his tricks, spinning an imaginary egg in the air and miming a juggling act. His mother chuckled softly, her laughter a balm to his soul, as she watched her son's enthusiasm fill the room with light.

A sudden cough escaped his mother's lips, halting Isaak mid-motion. Concern washed over him as he rushed to her side, his joy from moments before replaced with worry. He quickly fetched a cup of water, gently helping her to drink, his hands trembling slightly as he steadied the cup.

Kneeling beside her, Isaak took her hand in his, his voice soft and laced with emotion. "Mama," he murmured, "I worry for thee. Thy health... it troubles me so." His eyes searched hers, his heart heavy with the painful truth he could not ignore she was growing weaker, and it pained him deeply to witness it.

"I'll be fine, my dear Isaak," his mother said, her voice gentle but resolute. "Do not worry for me. Instead, keep thy focus on thy dream."

She paused, her gaze softening as she looked at her son. "Dost, thou know what I see within thy heart?"

Isaak shook his head slowly, his voice barely above a whisper. "No, Mama... What dost thou see?"

With a tender smile, his mother reached out, placing her hand gently upon his face. She looked deep into his eyes, her own filled with warmth and love. "I see the very embodiment of joy," she said softly. "I see a man of great spirit. I see my son. I see the beauty of life itself reflected in thee. That is what I see in thee, Isaak."

Isaak offered a faint smile, his emotions warring within him—sadness and joy locked in a bittersweet dance. "Mama," he murmured, his voice trembling, "how shall I go on if thou dost pass? How can my joy endure without thee?"

His mother's smile remained steadfast, and she gently placed her hand over Isaak's heart. "Fret not, my beloved child," she said softly. "For I shall always dwell here, within this heart of thine, which I cherish so dearly."

Her hand fell to his, and she gave it a gentle squeeze. "But now," she continued, her voice growing faint, "I feel weary. The day has taken much from me."

Isaak leaned forward and placed a tender kiss upon her cheek. "Rest well, Mama," he said lovingly. "I shall check on thee later." He rose quietly, his steps light as he left the room, carrying her words within him like a lantern against the dark.

Yenn offered one final, gentle smile as Isaak quietly departed her room.

Isaak then made his way to his own chamber, where a tall standing mirror awaited him. He paused before it, staring at his reflection with searching eyes. "I cannot see what thou dost see, Mother," he whispered, his voice heavy with sorrow. "All I see is a boy burdened by a deep and unshakable sadness."

His shoulders trembled as his emotions overwhelmed him, and he sank to his knees, tears streaming down his face. For several moments, he wept, his sobs echoing softly in the stillness of the room.

But after a time, he rose, wiping his tears with the back of his hand. Determined to find solace, Isaak ran from the house, his feet carrying him to his special place—a great, ancient tree that stood not far from his home. Its sprawling branches reached skyward, and beneath its shade, he sought comfort amidst the quiet embrace of nature.

Isaak climbed the tree with practiced ease, ascending to its highest branches where the view stretched far and wide. From this perch, he could see the kingdom's grand royal palace rising majestically in the distance.

As he gazed at its towering spires, his heart swelled with determination, and his dream burned brighter than ever. To become the royal jester—that was his goal. Not merely for the honor or the joy it would bring him, but for the hope it carried. If he could achieve such a position, his father could finally rest from his relentless toil, and perhaps his mother could receive the care she so desperately needed.

The thought filled Isaak with renewed purpose. This dream was not just his own; it was a way to bring light to his family's life. And from his place high in the tree, he vowed silently to do whatever it took to make it a reality.

Isaak's mind brimmed with fresh ideas for jokes and routines, each more creative than the last. But amidst the flurry of inspiration, a single, burning resolve took hold of him—his greatest plan yet. He would journey to the capital, to the grand royal palace, and claim the title of royal jester. In doing so, he would secure the help his mother so desperately needed and prove to his father that he was destined for more than just jesting.

Determined, Isaak rushed home, his heart pounding with anticipation. He filled a small bag with only the barest essentials and tied it securely to his late grandfather's sturdy walking stick. With his belongings prepared, he made his way to his mother's room one last time.

Kneeling by her bedside, he softly explained his plan, his voice steady yet tinged with emotion. His mother listened intently, her eyes shining with pride. She smiled, reaching out to hold his hand.

"Go, my dear Isaak," she said warmly.

"Be safe and follow thy heart. I wish thee all the best."

With her blessing, Isaak rose, kissed her hand gently, and turned to leave, his spirit aflame with purpose as he embarked on the journey that would change his life forever.

Isaak took a moment to say his heartfelt farewells to his sister, embracing her tightly before stepping away. With determination etched on his face, he made his way to the village center, his steps light but resolute.

Standing tall before the gathered villagers, he called out, "I bid thee all adieu! Mark my words, I shall become the royal jester—just you see!"

Some villagers exchanged skeptical glances and scoffed, dismissing his bold declaration as a fool's errand. But among them were those who believed parents and their wide-eyed children, and even a few of the village guards who had watched Isaak grow into the spirited young man he was.

These supporters called out words of encouragement, their voices tinged with emotion, and some shed quiet tears as they bid him farewell. Isaak smiled brightly, their belief in him a flame that would light his path. With a wave and a flourishing bow, he turned toward the road that led to the capital, his heart brimming with hope and determination.

Before departing the village, Isaak sought out his mentor, the wise and steadfast Henry. Finding the old man near the edge of the village, Isaak approached with a mixture of gratitude and solemnity in his heart.

"Sirrah Henry," he began, his voice steady but laced with emotion, "I am off to chase my dream. But before I go, I must ask thee a favor. Please, look after my family in my absence. They are my most cherished treasure in all the world... as art thou."

Henry's eyes softened, and he nodded, placing a firm hand on Isaak's shoulder. "Fear not, lad," he said kindly.

"Thy family shall be cared for, as though they were my own."

Isaak smiled, though his heart ached to leave, and bowed deeply to his mentor.

Henry pulled Isaak into a warm embrace, his voice steady but tinged with emotion as he said, "Go well, lad, and may fortune favor thee. But before thou leave, perhaps thou shouldst bid thy father farewell."

Isaak hesitated, his expression somber. "I fear that would not end well, Henry. He would only try to stop me." He paused, then reached into his bag and pulled out a folded letter, worn slightly from handling.

"But give him this, I beg thee. I wrote it before I made my decision to leave. Within, I've explained my plan and promised that one day, I shall return."

Henry accepted the letter with a nod, understanding the weight of Isaak's choice. With a final clasp of Henry's hand, Isaak turned and began his journey, the village slowly fading behind him as he set his sights on the royal palace and the dream that awaited him there.

CHAPTER THREE:
The Bond Forged in Twilight

Isaak, now far from the comforts of his home, had traveled more than a day's walk. In the distance, his village was no more than a faint memory on the horizon. Yet his resolve remained steadfast, his heart set on the capital and the dream that called him forward.

On the fourth day of his journey, as the sun dipped low and painted the road in hues of amber, Isaak's path was interrupted by the sound of coarse laughter. From the shadows of the trees, a group of rough-looking men emerged, their eyes gleaming with mischief.

"Oi, what have we here, lads?" one of them sneered, stepping forward with a wicked grin. "A lonesome jester wandering the king's roads!"

The others chuckled darkly, unsheathing their blades with a metallic hiss that seemed to echo through the stillness of the forest.

"Surely a fool like you's carrying somethin' of value," the leader continued, his tone dripping with menace. "Hand it over nice and easy, and we might just let you skip off with that silly grin still on your face."

Isaak's hand instinctively tightened around his grandfather's walking stick, his mind racing. Though fear pricked at the edges of his thoughts, he forced a smirk to his lips, determined not to let his tormentors see his unease. "Gentlemen," he began, his voice calm yet laced with mockery, "surely thou wouldst not stoop so low as to rob a mere jester? Pray, have ye no humor in your blackened hearts?"

The bandits, taken aback for only a moment, laughed once more, though their expressions turned colder. The stage was set, and Isaak knew he would have to rely on wit, resolve, and perhaps a touch of luck to escape their clutches unscathed.

Isaak, ever quick with his wits, responded to the threat with a sly grin. Reaching into his bag, he grabbed a handful of eggs and hurled them at the bandits, the fragile shells splattering yolk across their faces and clothing.

"Catch me if you can, knaves!" he shouted, spinning on his heels and bolting down the path, his heart pounding as his legs carried him faster than he thought possible. Behind him, the bandits roared in fury, shouting curses that echoed through the forest as they gave chase.

Twisting through the trees, Isaak's mind raced for a plan. Ahead, the sound of voices and movement caught his attention. Bursting into a clearing, he found himself face-to-face with another group of armed figures—a different band of cutthroats. Panic rose in his chest, but desperation drove him forward.

"Please, I beg of thee!" Isaak called out, dropping to his knees before their leader, a young woman with piercing eyes and a confident stance. She couldn't have been much older than he, yet she held an air of authority that silenced the others.

"What's this?" she asked with a smirk, tilting her head curiously. "A jester pleading for mercy? How amusing."

Isaak clasped his hands together, his voice earnest but hurried. "I am pursued by rogues most foul. Help me, and I swear to repay thy kindness!"

The woman's gaze lingered on him for a moment before she broke into a chuckle. "Very well, fool. I shall aid thee—but only if thou dost agree to owe me a favor. Do we have a bargain?"

With the sound of the pursuing bandits drawing closer, Isaak nodded fervently. "Aye, my lady, thou hast my word!"

The woman's grin widened, and with a wave of her hand, her crew stepped forward, ready to face the approaching danger. Isaak couldn't help but feel both relief and apprehension—he had escaped one peril, only to step into the unknown with this enigmatic leader who now held his fate in her hands.

The bandit leader, her sharp eyes glinting with determination, tossed a spare hatchet to Isaak. "Here, take this," she said firmly. "I'll not have thee standing defenseless while we fight!"

Isaak caught the weapon clumsily, nearly dropping it as he looked at her in alarm. "Uh... my lady, I fear I am no warrior. My talents lie more in jest and charm than in combat. Though," he added sheepishly, "I did spend some years as a guard, so I shall do my utmost for thee."

The woman smirked at his honest confession, crossing her arms as she watched him nervously juggle the hatchet. "Thy jesting days may aid thee yet," she teased, raising an eyebrow as he finally caught the weapon with surprising precision, gripping it like a seasoned fighter.

The sounds of footsteps and shouted threats broke their brief moment. The bandits chasing Isaak emerged from the shadows of the forest, their blades glinting menacingly in the dim light. Without hesitation, the woman gave a sharp whistle, rallying her crew.

"Ready thyself, jester," she said with a grin that carried both mischief and challenge. "Let us see if thy courage matches thy wit."

Isaak nodded; his nerves pushed aside by the thrill of the moment. As the two groups clashed, he threw himself into the fray, relying on the nimble acrobatics he had honed over the years. His flips, spins, and quick reflexes caught the rogues off guard, and he used the hatchet with surprising finesse.

Beside him, the woman fought like a tempest, her strikes swift and calculated, her movements a deadly dance. Isaak couldn't help but steal glances at her—how her fierce determination lit her face, how she moved with the grace of a predator. Despite having just met, their actions synchronized as though they had fought side by side for years.

When one of the attackers lunged at Isaak, she was there in an instant, felling the rogue with a single, well-placed blow. "Keep thy head, fool!" she barked with a smirk, her tone almost affectionate.

"And I'll keep my heart, if thou dost allow it!" Isaak quipped back, grinning despite the chaos around them.

Their combined effort was unstoppable. Bandit after bandit fell before their unlikely partnership, the rogues scattering in defeat. Isaak, catching his breath, looked over at the woman, her face still fierce but softened with the faintest smile of victory.

In that moment, as the adrenaline faded and he stood among the aftermath of their battle, he realized he was utterly captivated. The fire in her eyes, the strength in her stance—he was enamored, not just by her skill, but by the mystery and passion she carried. For once, he found himself at a loss for words, his heart racing not from danger, but from the beginnings of something far more profound.

Isaak bowed slightly, a gesture of gratitude as he spoke. "I thank thee again, my lady. Truly, thou hast been a light in this dark hour." He extended the hatchet back toward her, but she shook her head, a smirk playing on her lips.

"Nay, keep it, my funny friend," she replied. "These are dark times, and thou may yet have need of it."

Isaak paused before nodding, his grin returning. He tossed the hatchet lightly into the air, letting it spin before catching it with ease and sliding it into a makeshift holster at his side.

The woman raised an eyebrow, clapping her hands in mock applause. "It seems thou art incapable of resisting theatrics."

"Guilty as charged," Isaak admitted with a chuckle.

She laughed warmly and gestured for him to follow. "Come, join us at our camp. There are friends thou must meet."

The camp was nestled in a clearing, alive with the glow of a central fire. As they entered, she began introductions. "These are my men," she said, gesturing to the gathered group, each one offering a nod or a glance of acknowledgment. She pointed to a broad-shouldered man with a shrewd gaze. "David, the merchant, who keeps us well-supplied and shrewdly negotiates with the world."

Next, she indicated a tall woman with arms like tree trunks and a scar across her cheek. "Amelie, our berserker. None are fiercer in battle." Amelie gave Isaak a curt nod, her stern face betraying a flicker of curiosity.

A wiry man with sharp eyes and a satchel filled with vials and tools was introduced next. "Fredrick, the surgeon. He's patched us up more times than I can count." Fredrick waved absently, already busy inspecting his supplies.

Finally, her tone softened as she gestured to a younger boy, barely in his teens, sitting by the fire with a scowl on his face. "And this," she said with a chuckle, "is my little brother, Samuel."

Samuel glared at Isaak. "Keep away from my sister!" he demanded, his youthful voice full of misplaced authority.

The woman threw her head back and laughed, ruffling her brother's hair. "Pay him no mind," she said, amusement lighting her face. "He is rather overprotective, though I'm more than capable of fending for myself."

Isaak couldn't help but laugh with her, his earlier nerves melting away in the warmth of the group. "Fear not, Sirrah Samuel," Isaak said, bowing theatrically to the boy. "Thy sister's strength is evident. I would not dare to cross her!"

The group chuckled, even Samuel cracking a reluctant smile. Isaak felt a strange comfort in their company, a sense of belonging among this band of outlaws that he hadn't expected. The firelight danced on their faces, and as the evening carried on, he couldn't help but feel that his journey had taken a most curious and promising turn.

Isaak found himself captivated by the sound of her laughter. It was melodic, warm, and far more enchanting than he had anticipated. In his mind, a quiet yearning took root—he wanted to hear it again and again, to be the source of her joy like he had never desired before.

"May I ask thy name?" he said at last, breaking the comfortable silence between them. "I know thee only as the leader of this band of... cut-armed men." A playful smile tugged at his lips.

She chuckled softly at his jest, her confidence unwavering. "I am Raisa," she said, her voice carrying a softness that belied the strength in her gaze.

Isaak quickly slipped on his mask, hoping to conceal the blush rising to his cheeks. "Raisa," he repeated, as though savoring the sound. "I am Isaak, and it is a pleasure to meet thee."

The two fell into easy conversation, spending the rest of the day wandering the camp and speaking of anything that came to mind. Isaak shared tales of his family, speaking fondly of his mother's warmth, his sister's humor, and even his father's stern but loving nature. He painted vivid pictures of his hopes and dreams—the joy he wished to spread as a royal jester, the life he envisioned for his family, and the purpose that drove him forward.

Raisa, in turn, spoke with an openness Isaak hadn't expected. She told him of her past, of a family now lost save for Samuel, her fiercely protective younger brother. Her words were tinged with both pride and sorrow as she explained how they had turned to banditry—not out of malice, but necessity. The world had not been kind, and survival often demanded choices that weighed heavily on the soul.

As Isaak listened, he felt a growing respect for Raisa. Beneath her commanding presence lay a heart shaped by hardship, one that bore the weight of her people's well-being with quiet strength. He admired her resilience and the lengths she went to protect those she cared for.

By the time the sun began to set, casting the camp in hues of gold and crimson, Isaak realized that he had not only found an ally but also someone who intrigued him in ways he could scarcely describe. For the first time since leaving his village, he felt a spark of something new—a connection that might one day grow into something more.

As the evening deepened and the campfires flickered against the growing darkness, Isaak walked alongside Raisa to her tent. The air was cool, filled with the quiet hum of distant conversations and the occasional crackle of burning wood. At the entrance, he paused, turning to her with a smile. "I wish thee a good night, Raisa."

Before he could leave, she called out, her voice curious. "Isaak, if I may ask before you depart—how dost thou intend to become the royal jester? The king already has one."

Her question stopped him in his tracks. He hesitated, his usual quick wit faltering for a moment. "Truth be told," he admitted with a small shrug, "I shall figure it out when the time comes. Destiny, I've found, tends to reward boldness."

With a flourish of his hand, Isaak produced a single rose, as though it had materialized from thin air. He offered it to her with a theatrical bow, the grin beneath his mask unmistakable. "Until we meet again, Raisa," he said, his voice softer now. "I must continue my journey. There is no time for rest but know this—should thou ever find me and require a favor; I shall honor my word and do all within my power to help thee."

Raisa accepted the rose, her lips curving into a small, amused smile. "Ever the dramatist, Isaak."

He chuckled and then, as if remembering something, turned to her again. "Might I impose upon thee for one last favor? A horse, perchance? My legs grow weary, and the road ahead is long."

Raisa nodded, gesturing to a smaller horse tethered nearby. "This one we have no need of. Take her—she's swift, if a bit stubborn. I trust thou can handle her."

Isaak bowed deeply, placing his hand over his heart. "Thy generosity humbles me, my lady." He mounted the horse with practiced ease, giving Raisa one last glance as he adjusted his mask.

Their eyes met for a lingering moment, and then, with a playful salute, Isaak urged the horse forward, leaving the camp behind. As he rode off into the night, the rose still in Raisa's hand, he couldn't help but feel a sense of possibility blooming in his chest—one that extended far beyond his dream of becoming a royal jester.

Isaak rode onward along King's Road, the rhythmic clatter of his horse's hooves a steady companion to his thoughts. His hatchet rested securely in its sheath, a symbol of both protection and the resolve that fueled his journey. Determined as ever, he pressed forward, his sights set on his ultimate goal: the royal court and the title of royal jester.

As the days turned to weeks, Isaak encountered small villages nestled along the road. In each one, he paused to perform, setting up makeshift stages in bustling market squares or cozy inns. His antics—juggling, acrobatics, and tales filled with humor and whimsy—drew crowds of villagers who quickly filled his hat with coins. The laughter of children and the cheers of adults became a balm for his weary spirit, as well as a means to fund his journey.

But it was more than just survival; Isaak sought renown. He needed the whispers of his name to travel ahead of him, to fill the kingdom with tales of the wandering jester whose charm and skill were unmatched. Yet, despite his growing success, some villages met him with indifference, their people unaware of who he was or what he aimed to become. Isaak took it as a challenge, vowing to leave no corner of the realm untouched by his presence.

Not all his encounters were joyous. King's Road was fraught with peril, and Isaak found himself in the occasional skirmish with thieves and cutthroats who sought to relieve him of his earnings. With quick wit and quicker hands, he defended himself, his acrobatic prowess and his hatchet proving invaluable. Some battles were fought with steel, others with guile, but Isaak always emerged victorious, his resolve only strengthened by each confrontation.

With every village visited, every crowd entertained, and every danger overcome, Isaak felt his confidence grow. He was no longer just a dreamer; he was a man on a mission, carving his way toward the royal palace with laughter and determination as his guide. Months had passed since Isaak had left the comforts of his home. The journey had been long and arduous, yet his spirit remained unbroken. Though the capital loomed closer on the horizon, it was still a distant dream. Weary from travel, he arrived at a quaint little town nestled at the edge of a dense forest. Deciding it was a good place to rest and replenish his energy, Isaak wasted no time preparing to perform.

In the heart of the town square, he assembled a modest stage from crates and planks. Standing tall upon it, he addressed the gathering townsfolk with theatrical flair. "Hear me, good people! I am Isaak, the Jester of all Jesters! I proclaim myself the King of Fools, and to prove my title, I invite you to witness my unrivaled performance. Prepare to be dazzled and delighted by my prowess!"

With a dramatic flourish, Isaak produced his hatchet and a few eggs, juggling them with ease. His hands moved like lightning, and the objects seemed to dance in the air, capturing the crowd's attention. As he performed, Isaak spun a tale of adventure, regaling them with the story of a jester who bravely fought a band of fearsome outlaws and emerged victorious.

"The final bandit was a towering brute, as massive as an ogre!" he exclaimed, widening his arms for emphasis. "But the King of Fools did not waver, for he had courage in his heart and wit as sharp as his blade!" He recounted his encounter with Raisa and her band, weaving their alliance into the tale. Of course, he embellished it with humorous exaggerations, painting Raisa as the bold Bandit Queen and himself as the heroic fool whose antics turned the tide.

"And so," Isaak declared, tossing the eggs high and catching them deftly, "the Bandit Queen and the King of Fools defeated the great ogre, and they lived happily ever after!"

The square erupted with cheers and laughter. The children clapped with glee, their eyes alight with wonder, while the adults marveled at Isaak's acrobatic feats and clever humor. In that moment, the burdens of their daily lives seemed to fade, replaced by the joy Isaak brought with his performance.

As Isaak took his final bow, he felt a surge of pride. These moments of connection, the laughter and the applause, were why he continued his journey. With every town he visited, his reputation grew, and so too did his dream of standing before the king as the one true King of Fools.

To close his performance, Isaak decided to make one final joke about the current royal jester. With a sly grin, he said, "Ah, the royal jester—surely a man of great wit... or so they say. But I hear he couldn't juggle his way out of a paper bag!"

The crowd erupted in laughter, most of them enjoying the jest at the expense of the royal court. However, a few in the crowd seemed taken aback, some even frowning at the audacity of his words. Isaak, ever the performer, shrugged off the few disapproving glances, his smile never faltering as he gathered his coins. A good jest, after all, was a reflection of his wit, and he knew that humor often found its sharpest edge in truth.

After collecting his earnings, Isaak made his way to the local inn. The smell of warm bread and the sound of crackling fire welcomed him as he entered. He paid for a small room, one with a simple bed and a window that looked out over the town square. Sighing with relief, he unpacked his few belongings, stretching his weary limbs.

As the sun dipped below the horizon, Isaak sat at the small writing desk in the corner of the room. He took out a piece of parchment and a quill, his thoughts filled with the day's events. He wrote to his family, detailing his travels, the excitement of his performances, and how each village brought him closer to his dream. He shared the joy of his journey, but most importantly, he spoke of a new and unexpected feeling that had taken root in his heart.

"I have met someone," he wrote, pausing for a moment before continuing. "A woman whose strength and spirit have touched me in ways I never expected. Her name is Raisa, and though our paths are still uncertain, I find myself thinking of her often. She has stolen my heart in ways that even my best jokes could never express."

With a contented sigh, Isaak folded the letter and sealed it, feeling the weight of his journey and his emotions settle within him. The road ahead was still long, but tonight, as he lay his head down to rest, he knew that he was one step closer to both his dream and his heart's desire.

CHAPTER FOUR:
A Brotherhood Formed

Isaak woke suddenly to the sound of wood splintering—a loud crash that shook the inn. His eyes snapped open, and without hesitation, he scrambled out of bed, pulling on his clothes and grabbing his hatchet. His heart raced as his senses sharpened.

He heard the sounds of shouting, a harsh and menacing voice, followed by the sobs of someone in distress. With a swift motion, Isaak placed his mask over his face, the familiar comfort of it settling over his features, hiding his emotions behind the painted grin.

Without a moment's hesitation, he ran down the stairs, his feet pounding against the wooden floor. As he entered the main hall of the inn, the scene before him was one of chaos. Four large, heavily armed men towered over the proprietor, a frail and elderly man who was trembling in fear.

"Give us all your gold, old man!" one of the bandits shouted, his voice thick with menace. "Or you won't live to see the dawn!"

The old man's voice quivered as he pleaded, "I... I have no gold! Please, leave me be..."

Isaak's blood boiled at the sight of the elderly man being shoved to the ground, his tears mixing with the dust on the floor. This was more than Isaak could stand. His heart pounded in his chest as a fierce determination overtook him.

He stepped forward with the swiftness of a shadow, his hatchet raised in a fluid motion. With a deadly accuracy honed through years of practice, Isaak hurled the hatchet at the man who had been threatening the innkeeper. The weapon struck with a sickening thud, embedding itself in the bandit's skull.

The remaining three men froze, their eyes widening as they realized the jester was no mere performer.

Isaak stood tall, his stance steady and firm. His mask, though painted with a smile, reflected the resolve in his eyes.

"I'd suggest leaving him alone," Isaak called out, his voice cold and unwavering. "Or you'll contend with me."

He clenched his fists, muscles tensing in preparation for the fight ahead. His acrobatics might win him applause, but tonight, it would be his fighting spirit that would see him through. The three bandits, now uncertain, began to hesitate, sensing that they had underestimated this jester far more than they should have.

The three remaining armed men snarled at Isaak, fury in their eyes. The leader of the group, a broad-shouldered brute with a scarred face, growled, "Kill that jester, boys! He killed Gary!"

Isaak didn't flinch. He knew this fight wasn't one he could talk his way out of. In a fluid motion, he sprang into action, his body twisting and turning with the grace of a seasoned acrobat. He danced around the bandits, dodging their clumsy strikes and spilling mugs of ale across their chests. With each flip and somersault, he made them look like complete fools.

The men growled and cursed, their faces splattered with eggs he had thrown in their direction, only adding to their humiliation. Isaak's movements were lightning-fast, and he used every trick up his sleeve, blending humor and agility with deadly intent. When the time came, he grabbed his hatchet, swinging it with precision and bringing down one of the men with a swift blow.

But the fight wasn't easy. Several times, Isaak found himself on the defensive, barely dodging a blade or a fist that came far too close for comfort. His heart raced with adrenaline, but his determination was stronger than his fear. He would not lose to these ruffians—not in his pursuit of his dream, and certainly not in front of an innocent man.

At last, only one man remained—a towering figure, scarred and vicious. He sneered down at Isaak, cracking his knuckles in anticipation.

"I do not like you, clown!" the giant roared, his massive fist crashing into Isaak's stomach, knocking the wind from his lungs.

Isaak gasped for breath; his vision blurred for a moment. "You need not like me," he wheezed, fighting to regain his footing.

In a swift, desperate move, Isaak grabbed a nearby mug of ale and splashed it directly into the large man's eyes. The man staggered back, growling in frustration as he rubbed at his face. Isaak saw his opportunity.

"You need only to surrender," Isaak said, his voice steely.

Isaak launched himself at the man, landing a flurry of punches and kicks, using his speed and agility to wear down the giant. Each strike landed with a satisfying thud, and the man's attempts to retaliate grew slower and more desperate.

"You are one tough man, Sirrah," Isaak muttered, admiration mingling with exhaustion as he landed a final punch to the man's jaw, knocking him out cold.

Isaak dropped to his knees, panting heavily, sweat dripping down his face. His body screamed for rest, but his mission was far from over.

"Innkeeper," Isaak croaked, his voice hoarse, "may I have a cup of water, if possible?"

He tried to smile, but it quickly turned into a chuckle that fizzled out. As he sat there, weary and bloodied, his head spun, and with a sigh, Isaak finally collapsed to the floor, his body unable to fight off the exhaustion any longer.

The innkeeper carefully helped Isaak to his room, his rough hands supporting the jester's weary form as they ascended the stairs. Once inside, the innkeeper gently tended to Isaak's wounds, wiping away the blood and patching up the bruises with an experienced hand. Isaak gratefully accepted the care, his body heavy with exhaustion from the fight. He fell into a deep, restful sleep, the events of the night fading into dreams.

When Isaak awoke, he found the innkeeper sitting beside him, a humble but warm smile on his face. The old man's eyes shone with gratitude. "I thank ye again, Isaak," the innkeeper said, his voice thick with emotion. "Ye saved me, and the inn. How can I ever repay ye?"

Isaak smiled faintly, though his tiredness still hung heavily on him. He shook his head, refusing the offer. "I shan't take your money. That is yours, not mine," Isaak said with a wave of his hand. "What I did, I did because it was right."

The innkeeper hesitated, then nodded in understanding. Isaak, always a man of honor, wasn't about to take gold for something that felt more like destiny.

After some moments, Isaak pulled out his coin purse, paying for his room. "Also, I have a favor to ask," Isaak said as he handed the innkeeper a small letter. "Could you have this sent for me? To my family."

"Of course, lad. Consider it done," the innkeeper said, tucking the letter into his coat. He clapped Isaak on the shoulder and watched him leave, hoping that Isaak's journey would bring him the success he so clearly desired.

With a final farewell to the innkeeper, Isaak continued his travels. The road ahead seemed endless, but he pressed on with unwavering determination. He had finally made it to the capital—his dream was now within his grasp. After so many months of traveling, through the bandits, the battles, and the hardships, Isaak could hardly believe he was standing in front of the massive gates of the capital city. The stone walls loomed before him, towering and impressive.

He approached the guards at the gate, standing tall despite the weariness that still clung to him. With his hatchet at his side and his mask hiding his expression, he spoke with a firm, confident tone. "I am Isaak, the jester of all jesters."

The guards exchanged skeptical glances. One of them, a gruff man with a thick beard, looked him over and said, "A jester, eh? We already have a royal jester, but you may enter the city. We have nothing against thee."

Isaak nodded, feeling both a sense of relief and a renewed determination as the gates creaked open, allowing him entry. The path to the royal palace still stretched ahead, but now Isaak knew he was one step closer to achieving his dream. He smiled behind his mask, his heart pounding with anticipation. His journey was far from over, but the capital was the next step on the path that would lead him to the throne of fools.

Isaak entered the capital city with wide eyes, taking in the grandeur of the towering stone buildings, the bustling marketplace, and the lavishness that surrounded him. He moved through the crowded streets, weaving through throngs of people, trying to gather information and figure out his next move. He spoke with the townsfolk, learning what he could about the royal jester who currently held the position at court. What he discovered wasn't encouraging—no one seemed to have much love for the man. In fact, they found him a bore, stiff and unremarkable. The only person who seemed to appreciate his presence was the queen herself, who favored him for one simple reason: the royal jester never made jokes at her expense.

Isaak grinned beneath his mask, seeing an opportunity unfold before him. If he could get the queen to laugh, to see his talent, perhaps he could make his way into the palace, impress the king and queen, and claim the title of royal jester for himself. But first, he needed to figure out how to get an audience with the royal couple.

He couldn't just walk in and demand a meeting. No, he'd need to be clever about it.

As Isaak pondered his next move, he wandered deeper into the city, eyes scanning for any possible opportunities. That's when he saw him—a young pickpocket, slipping through the crowd with an almost imperceptible grace. Isaak's sharp eyes caught the movement, and with a smirk, he approached the thief. "You know, it would be less obvious when you steal if you didn't make such a guilty face," Isaak called out, his voice lighthearted, yet knowing.

The young man jumped, his hand quickly slipping the stolen goods back into his pocket, startled by Isaak's keen observation. "I do not know what you mean, jester. I'm no thief," he protested, attempting to feign innocence.

Isaak raised an eyebrow, grinning wider. "I may be a fool, but I ain't a fool. You're as guilty as a rat in a cheese shop." His voice was playful but firm, and the thief couldn't help but chuckle at the jest.

"I—uh... I suppose you're right," the young man muttered, glancing around nervously. "You're pretty sharp for a fool."

Isaak chuckled, stepping closer. "A fool who knows when to be observant. You know, a thief could use a bit of subtlety. You might want to work on that." He eyed the young man more carefully now, studying him as he tried to hide his loot. "So, what's your name, thief?"

The young man hesitated for a moment, then shrugged. "Jeremy. What's it to you?"

Isaak raised an eyebrow. "Peculiar name," he said with a teasing tone, and the young man looked at him, confused.

"Is it? I'd say Isaak is peculiar," Jeremy replied, and a grin spread across his face. They both laughed, and in that moment, an unlikely friendship began to form.

Over the next few days, Isaak and Jeremy became inseparable. They pulled pranks together, causing chaos in the streets, laughing as they danced around the city causing mischief wherever they went. Jeremy, for all his skill as a pickpocket, had a good heart. He didn't take from people who couldn't afford it, and he found himself drawn to Isaak's sense of humor and his infectious joy. Isaak, in turn, admired Jeremy's quick wit and street-smart ways.

Soon, Jeremy was helping Isaak with his performances, using his thieving skills to assist in Isaak's acts. He became Isaak's right-hand man, passing him props and even helping him set up his stage. With Jeremy's help, Isaak's performances grew more elaborate, and their antics on the streets began to draw larger crowds. Their partnership felt effortless, like they had been working together for years.

One night, as they performed together under the glow of the city's lanterns, Isaak couldn't help but feel a surge of excitement. He was closer than ever to his dream, and with Jeremy by his side, he was certain that soon he would find a way to win the favor of the queen—and maybe even the king—and take his place as the royal jester.

Isaak beamed with excitement as he and Jeremy continued their antics, performing in the streets and laughing at the chaos they stirred up. "See? Isn't this more fun than stealing?" Isaak asked, watching as the crowd erupted into applause after another of their spectacular tricks.

Jeremy grinned, but a glint of mischief still sparkled in his eyes. "You're not wrong, but I still prefer the thrill of the pickpocket," he admitted, a smirk tugging at his lips. "It's quicker, more subtle, and the rewards are immediate."

Isaak raised an eyebrow, intrigued. "You're a bold one, Jeremy. I'll give you that. But teach me how to do it—let's see if I can master this 'art' of yours."

And so, Jeremy took it upon himself to teach Isaak the finer points of pickpocketing. It didn't take long for the jester to pick up the skill, his quick hands and acrobatic moves making him a natural. The pair began to target various nobles in the city, swiping their coin purses and valuables with the grace of seasoned thieves. However, Isaak's heart wasn't as ruthless as Jeremy's. Instead of keeping everything to themselves, the two would sneakily distribute their stolen wealth to the poor, making sure the city's most downtrodden had a little something to brighten their day.

At times, they kept a little for themselves—just enough to sustain their mischief and adventures. Isaak was never one to hoard riches; he always saw the world as a stage for laughter, fun, and camaraderie. But as they carried out their antics, he began to realize something more important than any wealth: the bond he shared with Jeremy.

Their friendship had grown into something deeper—a brotherhood. Isaak saw Jeremy as the brother he never had. They fought together, laughed together, and worked side by side in ways that felt natural, as though they were destined to be partners in crime. Their trust in one another was unshakable, and with each passing day, Isaak felt more and more grateful for the thief at his side.

In return, Jeremy had grown fond of Isaak too. He admired Isaak's heart and the way he always looked out for the less fortunate. Isaak's joy was contagious, and despite the rebellious life they led, Jeremy found himself feeling a sense of fulfillment he had never experienced before.

Together, they were unstoppable—two outcasts in a city of wealth and power, making their own rules, stealing from the rich, and giving to the poor. Their laughter echoed through the streets as they pulled off daring heists, and in the moments when they paused to catch their breath, they shared stories, dreams, and a bond that neither would trade for anything in the world.

Through their friendship, Isaak realized that no matter where his journey took him, it was the connections he made along the way that truly mattered. And in Jeremy, he had found a true companion—a brother who would stand by him, come what may.

CHAPTER FIVE:
The Warrior and The Jester

Isaak sat beside Jeremey one evening, a rare quiet moment in the midst of their usual hustle and bustle. The streets were alive with the sounds of the city, but for once, Isaak seemed lost in his thoughts. He turned to Jeremey, his voice soft and full of emotion. "I've told you about my family," Isaak began, his eyes distant, "and how they would accept you as one of their own. They'd welcome you like a true member."

Jeremey raised an eyebrow but said nothing, knowing Isaak had more to say. Isaak's gaze drifted to the horizon, where the evening sun painted the sky in hues of orange and purple. "But there's more..." Isaak continued; his voice tinged with affection. "There's someone I can't stop thinking about."

Of course, Jeremey already knew. Isaak had mentioned her time and time again. Raisa. The bandit leader, the woman who had stolen his heart. Isaak spoke of her with such reverence, it was as if she were a legend in his eyes. Jeremey could feel the shift in the air when Isaak spoke her name, as if the very mention of her brought light to the room.

But after weeks of hearing his friend speak about her, Jeremey's patience began to wane. "If you speak about her one more time," Jeremey warned, half-joking, "I swear, I'll yell. I'm not saying you can't talk about her, but I think I've heard enough. You've met her once, Isaak. How are you so sure about her?"

Isaak paused for a moment, and then, without a word, he removed his mask. For the first time in their friendship, he allowed Jeremey to see his face completely—no tricks, no theatrics, just Isaak. His expression was serious, vulnerable in a way he rarely allowed himself to be.

"I'm sure of you, my friend... my brother," Isaak replied, his voice steady but filled with emotion. His gaze softened as he looked at Jeremey, a warmth in his eyes that made the thief pause. "What I see in Raisa is something I've never seen before. Whenever I get into a fight, whenever I feel like I'm about to lose myself, I think of her. And it fills me with a feeling I can't explain. A kind of strength, a reason to keep going. When I think of her, I feel like I'm not just fighting for myself, but for something more."

Jeremey listened, his previous irritation melting away. Isaak's words were sincere, raw in a way that made him understand. He leaned back, crossing his arms, trying to put himself in his friend's shoes. "So... what would you do if you saw her again?" he asked, genuinely curious.

Isaak hesitated, his eyes falling to the ground as if searching for the right words. "I don't know," he admitted. "If I were to see her again, I don't think I'd have any words for her, no grand gestures. I would just want to see her smile. To hear her laugh. That's all I want. To bring her joy, the way she's brought it to me."

The air between them was quiet for a moment, and for the first time, Jeremey understood the depth of Isaak's feelings. It wasn't just infatuation. It was something deeper—something pure, almost innocent. Isaak wasn't looking for anything grand from Raisa. He simply wanted to see her happy.

"That sounds like love," Jeremey said quietly, a hint of amusement in his voice.

Isaak smiled, a small, wistful smile that tugged at his heart. "Maybe it is," he said, his voice barely above a whisper. "But I'm not in a rush to label it. I just know I want her to be happy."

Jeremey sat back, a thoughtful expression on his face. Despite his teasing, he couldn't help but admire the way Isaak's heart remained open, even in a world that was often harsh and unforgiving. His loyalty to his family, his deep affection for Raisa—it was all part of the same person: a fool who had the courage to care deeply, no matter the cost.

"Alright, Isaak," Jeremey said with a soft chuckle, "I get it. I just hope that when you meet her again, you don't forget that I still want to hear about your adventures. Even without all the mushy stuff."

Isaak laughed, the tension easing between them. "I'll try," he promised, his smile returning as he put his mask back on. "But no guarantees."

In that moment, Isaak realized how lucky he was to have someone like Jeremey by his side—a true brother who would listen, even when his antics became too much. And though the road ahead was uncertain, with his heart full of dreams and his brother beside him, Isaak felt ready for whatever came next.

Jeremey's grin widened as he leaned back, his arms crossed casually. "Brother," he said with a mischievous glint in his eye, "you may yet have the chance to meet her again."

Isaak's heart skipped a beat, his eyes lighting up at the possibility. "What do you mean?" he asked eagerly, unable to mask the sudden rush of hope that surged through him.

Jeremey leaned in a little closer, lowering his voice with playful secrecy. "I may or may not have spotted someone matching her description the other day," he teased, his tone full of mischief.

Isaak's breath caught in his chest, and he leaned forward, his hands gripping the edge of the table as if afraid the moment might slip away if he didn't hold on tight. "Where? When? Tell me everything!"

Jeremey chuckled at Isaak's sudden enthusiasm, clearly enjoying the effect his words had on his friend. "Easy there, Jester. No need to get too excited. It wasn't much—just a glance, but she fit the description. Dark hair, a warrior's stance, and that fire in her eyes that I swear I've seen before. I saw her in the market, talking to a few merchants. I didn't stick around, but trust me, I'm pretty sure it was her."

Isaak's heart raced, his mind already running wild with possibilities. He could hardly believe it—after everything, after all the time that had passed, it seemed like fate might just be giving him a second chance. "Where did you see her? Can you take me there?"

Jeremey raised an eyebrow, his expression turning more serious. "I can't guarantee she'll still be there. But if you want to go looking, we can try. Just don't get your hopes up too much. She's not the kind of person who stays in one place for long, I'd wager."

Isaak nodded, a sense of urgency building in his chest. He had to find her, to see her again, to know if the connection he felt was as real as he remembered. "Then let's go," he said with determination in his voice. "I've come this far. I won't stop now."

Jeremey gave him an amused look. "You're a man on a mission, aren't you? Alright, Jester. Let's see where this wild goose chase takes us."

And with that, Isaak felt his heart lift once more, the possibility of finding Raisa—of seeing her smile, of hearing her laugh—filling him with a sense of purpose he hadn't felt in a long time. Whatever challenges lay ahead, he knew he had to try. For her. Jeremey led Isaak through the bustling marketplace, his eyes scanning the crowds as he pointed toward the grocer's stall. "She was around here, somewhere," he said, a glint of mischief in his eyes. "Now, remember what I told you. You can't just walk up and blurt out 'Hey, remember me?' though you might want to. Take your time."

Isaak stopped in his tracks, a nervous laugh escaping him. "What should I say, Jeremey? I mean, this is someone I—" His words faltered, his heart pounding in his chest as the thought of seeing Raisa again overwhelmed him. "I can't just go up and say that, can I?"

Jeremey chuckled, giving him a sly grin. "When you love someone, anything is possible. But maybe don't start with 'Hey, remember me?' Try something smoother. Show her you've thought about this moment."

Isaak took a deep breath, absorbing the advice, his nerves still buzzing as they made their way closer to the grocer's stall. He could see the familiar figures among the crowd—busy shoppers, children running, carts being pushed. But there, standing tall among them, was Raisa. His heart skipped a beat.

Her hair, dark red and flowing, caught the sunlight, and Isaak could already see the strength in her posture.

Her tall, muscular frame only seemed to have grown stronger since their last encounter. The sight of her brought memories rushing back—of their time together, their shared battle, and the laughter they'd exchanged.

Isaak's mind wandered for a moment. He imagined walking up to her, pulling her close, and pressing his lips against hers in a passionate kiss. The thought of holding her again felt so real, so close. But he snapped back to reality, shaking his head. He couldn't let his emotions take over—not just yet. He had to be calm, composed.

With newfound resolve, Isaak stepped forward. He approached her slowly, his heart pounding in his chest, and when he was right behind her, he cleared his throat softly. "Hello, my lady," he said, his voice steady but filled with warmth. "I do hope you remember me."

He bowed, as any good jester would, and with a flourish of his hand, he produced a rose from his sleeve, holding it out to her. His sleight of hand was smooth, practiced, and his gesture was one of both humor and affection.

Raisa turned at the sound of his voice, and her face broke into a smile that made Isaak's heart flutter. "Of course I remember you," she said, her voice light and musical. "My funny little friend. How fare thee?"

Isaak couldn't help but smile at the sound of her laugh, that same joy and warmth he remembered so clearly. "I fare well, my lady, better now that I see you again."

Her eyes twinkled as she glanced at the rose in his hand. "You always know how to make me smile, don't you?" she teased, taking the flower with a playful grin.

Isaak's heart soared. Maybe this time, things will be different. Maybe this time, he wouldn't have to walk away.

Isaak stood before Raisa, his heart racing as he greeted her. "How fare thee, my lady Raisa?" he asked, his voice filled with both respect and affection.

Raisa's expression softened as she smiled at him. "I am no longer a bandit, Isaak," she said, her tone steady but with a hint of pride. "I've become a mercenary now, and so has my crew. We are here in the capital to rest and gather supplies. We've agreed to help the king with his current campaign against a rival kingdom."

Isaak's ears perked up at the mention of the king and the upcoming siege. "A campaign, you say. What castle are you besieging?" he asked, eager for any chance to get closer to her.

Raisa's eyes darkened slightly as she spoke of the mission. "The castle we're going to besiege was stolen by the kingdom of Jovia. The king has asked us to take it back, offering a good amount of coin for our trouble. We've agreed, of course," she explained.

Isaak saw an opportunity—one he couldn't let slip by. He felt a burning desire to be near her again, to fight alongside her as they had done before. Without hesitation, he asked, "Would you allow me to join you? I would be honored to fight by your side once again."

Raisa's face lit up with a smile, and Isaak's heart seemed to skip a beat. "I longed to fight beside you again, my funny jester," she said, her words like music to his ears. The warmth of her smile made him feel as though he had found his place beside her.

Isaak's voice became softer, more earnest. "Think of this as me honoring the promise I made to you, my lady. I shall follow you wherever you lead."

Her smile grew wider, and she nodded. "Then it's settled. Welcome back, Isaak. I'm glad you're with us."

Isaak's chest swelled with happiness. He would do anything for her—fight beside her, support her, and, perhaps, in time, win her heart. His resolve had never been clearer.

Isaak, feeling an overwhelming sense of joy, decided it was time to introduce Raisa to his newfound brother, Jeremey. With a warm smile, he gestured to the young man standing beside him. "This is Jeremey, my brother," Isaak said, a deep sense of camaraderie in his voice. Jeremey returned the smile, giving a friendly wave as he stepped forward to greet her.

Raisa's eyes glinted with curiosity as she met Isaak's companion, and with a simple nod, she acknowledged him. "A pleasure to meet you, Jeremey," she said, her voice as confident as ever.

Isaak, feeling proud, then turned to show her something else. From his side, he pulled out the hatchet she had once given him, now proudly painted in the vibrant colors of a jester. "This is the hatchet you gave me," he explained with a grin. "It's become my own, adorned with the jesters' colors, just like my heart. I've come to treasure it."

Raisa's gaze softened, and she took a step closer to admire the transformation. "It suits you well, Isaak," she remarked, her tone touched with approval.

As the night went on, the three of them sat around the fire, exchanging stories, laughter, and plans. Isaak and Raisa spoke late into the night, sharing stories of their lives, their pasts, their ambitions. With each passing moment, Isaak felt himself drawn to her more than ever before. He cherished every laugh, every glance, every word she spoke.

When it was time to part ways, Isaak walked with her back to her camp, and he once again greeted her band of mercenaries, each one offering their own hearty nod or brief exchange. It wasn't long before Isaak found himself standing before her brother, Samuel, who now regarded him with a warmer gaze than the first time they had met. The tension between them had eased, and Samuel gave

Isaak a more genuine, if not entirely approving, nod of acknowledgment.

Isaak smiled back, feeling the sense of unity growing among them all. The night was spent in good company, and Isaak couldn't help but feel that he had found a place with Raisa and her crew—a place he could proudly call home, at least for the time being. Their conversation flowed effortlessly, each word spoken with ease, and as the night wore on, Raisa invited Isaak into her tent. The warmth of the firelight and the quiet serenity of the night filled the space between them. As the hours passed, their laughter echoed, light and free, until a sense of joy took over. Isaak, in his playful way, caught her hand and with a mischievous grin, led her into a dance.

"I hear this is how they dance at the royal balls," he said, his voice teasing as he took her hand and cupped it gently, guiding her into a waltz. With no music to accompany them, Isaak hummed a soft tune, his steps light and graceful as he swirled them both across the floor of the tent.

Raisa's laugh was a melody in itself, and she followed his movements with ease, her eyes twinkling with a mix of amusement and admiration.

As they danced, Isaak found the words he had longed to say. "I think of you often, Raisa. Ever since our first meeting, you've invaded my thoughts and my heart. You've stolen a treasure very dear to me."

Raisa smiled softly at his words, her cheeks turning a gentle shade of crimson. She held his gaze, and for a moment, the world outside of them seemed to disappear. Then, in a quiet voice, she spoke, her words echoing the ones his mother had once said to him—words he had never forgotten.

"Isaak, my funny little jester," she said, her tone tender, "I too cherish your heart. It is now my most cherished treasure. But do you know what I see within your heart and eyes?"

Isaak's breath caught in his chest as she leaned closer, her voice full of warmth and certainty.

"I see the very embodiment of joy. I see a man of great spirit. I see a jester of great esteem. I see the beauty of life itself reflected in thee. That is what I see in thee, Isaak."

Her words, so much like his mother's, filled him with an overwhelming sense of wonder. He stood still, his heart racing, as he searched her eyes, seeing the truth of her words reflected back at him. In that moment, Isaak knew he had found something rare and beautiful—a connection unlike any other.

Isaak, overwhelmed with emotion, stopped dancing as a tear slid down his cheek. His voice faltered as he spoke, "I'm sorry... it's just that my mother said something very similar."

Raisa, noticing the depth of his sorrow, gently pulled him into her arms. "I hope she's alright, Isaak. I haven't seen my family in years either. I understand the ache of missing them."

She looked into his eyes, her gaze softening with empathy and something deeper. The moment felt heavy with unspoken words and shared pain. Then, without another word, Raisa moved closer and pressed her lips to his.

The kiss was tender at first, but it quickly deepened, an outpouring of longing and affection. Isaak held her tightly, his heart racing, as if every kiss, every touch was telling her everything he couldn't express with words.

When they finally parted, breathless, Isaak whispered, "I love thee, Raisa."

Raisa smiled, her heart full, and kissed him again. "And I love thee, Isaak. You are my jester, my funny little jester, and I love thee with all my heart. You say I stole your heart, but it was you who, in truth, stole mine."

The night was filled with a quiet, undeniable passion, as the two of them explored their love for each other. They kissed, touched, and shared moments that felt timeless, a connection that neither had expected, but both had longed for. The world outside seemed to fade, leaving just the two of them—entwined in each other's arms, basking in the warmth of their love.

Isaak held Raisa close as they lay together, the warmth of their bodies mingling beneath the covers. He spoke softly, his voice filled with hope and sincerity.

"After I help you take back that castle, will you help me with my dream?"

Raisa, looking into his eyes with a smile that spoke volumes, nodded. "Of course, Isaak. Just as you've done so much for me, I'll do anything for you."

They stayed in each other's arms, drifting into a peaceful sleep, the night filled with a quiet sense of contentment.

As the first light of day broke, they awoke and got dressed. Isaak helped Raisa prepare, and soon they were standing before the rest of her crew. Isaak spoke with determination, addressing the group. "Now is the time to take back Castle Jezik from the Jovian's."

The crew roared with excitement, their spirits high and their anticipation palpable. Isaak, ever the performer, lightened the mood with his usual humor. As they mounted their horses and began the journey toward the castle, he told jokes and funny stories to keep morale high. His wit was infectious, and even in the face of an impending battle, the group found themselves laughing, their spirits lifted by his antics. Isaak's presence seemed to make everything feel lighter, as if, no matter the outcome of the battle, they could face it together united and joyful.

CHAPTER SIX:
Siege of Castle Jezik

The sun hung low over the horizon, casting an amber glow across the rolling hills as Isaak and his newfound comrades approached Castle Jezik. The fortress loomed ahead; its stone walls etched with the scars of past battles. The sound of clattering hooves and armor echoed through the air, blending with the rustling of the wind as the mercenaries and their allies gathered in formation.

Isaak rode at the front, his heart pounding not from fear, but from the anticipation of the battle ahead. This was more than just a fight for a castle—it was a chance to prove himself, to stand beside the woman he loved, and to honor the promise he made.

With a wink to Rasia, who rode beside him, he raised his voice, cutting through the tension that gripped the group. "Alright, my friends," Isaak called, "it's time to show these Jovian's what happens when they steal from the wrong kingdom!" His words were met with laughter, the group's spirits lifting as his humor spread like wildfire.

The gates of Castle Jezik stood before them, waiting to be reclaimed. And Isaak, the jester, was ready to play his part in a battle like no other. Isaak and his comrades charged forward with all the fury of a storm, smashing through the castle gates and clashing with the Jovian defenders. The air was thick with the sounds of steel meeting steel, and Isaak felt his heart race as he narrowly dodged a blow that would've ended him. But with Rasia and Jeremey at his side, he found his rhythm—together, they moved like a well-oiled machine, cutting through their enemies with precision and camaraderie.

The battle was fierce, with the three of them fending off wave after wave of attackers, but eventually, the castle was theirs once more. The Jovian's had been driven back; their forces decimated. Yet, amid the smoke and chaos, one final figure stood—massive, covered in scars, and towering over the trio. With a voice like a growl from the depths of the earth, he bellowed, "Who do you think you are, taking my castle from me? Do you know who I am?" The man yelled "I am Joffa the wise."

Isaak wiped the sweat from his brow and grinned, taking in the sight of the monstrous figure before him. The man's sheer size was enough to intimidate anyone, but Isaak couldn't help himself. His laughter erupted, breaking the tension of the moment. "I was sure you'd be Joffa the Mountain with your size!" he said between fits of laughter, much to Jeremey's exasperation.

"Now is not the time to laugh, friend," Jeremey warned, his voice tinged with concern.

But Isaak couldn't help it. The name "Joffa the Wise" seemed so ridiculous coming from such a hulking brute. The jovial jester fought to compose himself but found the humor in the situation too much to ignore. This would be a battle to remember, but it seemed, at least for now, laughter was the best weapon he had.

Once those words were uttered Joffa with anger apparent swung a large axe that Isaak barely dodged.

As soon as Joffa's furious words left his lips, he swung his massive axe with a terrifying roar. Isaak barely managed to dodge, his heart racing as the blade cleaved the air just inches from him. His grin, however, didn't fade.

"On second thought, not such a ridiculous name," Isaak quipped, dodging another wild swing. His acrobatics kept him light on his feet, dancing circles around Joffa, who was quickly losing patience.

The battle raged on, Isaak's agility pitting him against Joffa's brute strength. All the while, Isaak hurled insults, and even eggs, at his opponent, each one landing with a satisfying splat. "You know, for someone who calls themselves wise, you don't seem that wise," he taunted, a mischievous glint in his eye.

Rasia and Jeremey watched from the sidelines, keeping a cautious distance. Jeremey raised an eyebrow. "Should we help our jester?"

Rasia shook her head, her gaze never leaving Isaak. "No, he doesn't need it. I know my love, and he can handle himself."

The two watched as Isaak continued to mock Joffa, dancing just out of range of the brutal swings. Joffa's anger grew with each word Isaak spat, his face turning an even deeper shade of red with each insult.

"Why won't you just stay still and die, clown?" Joffa bellowed, his fury escalating. With every swing of his axe, the ground trembled, but Isaak was relentless, moving faster than the beast could swing.

Then, in a flash of inspiration, Isaak saw his moment. As Joffa swung once more, Isaak ducked and with a swift, calculated movement, tripped the giant into a deep pit that had been hidden in the rubble. Joffa's roar of surprise was cut short as he tumbled into the hole, the clash of his armor echoing as he fell.

Isaak stood at the edge of the pit, panting with laughter and exhaustion. "Guess you weren't as wise as you thought, Joffa!" he called down, wiping an imaginary bead of sweat from his brow. "Woah looks like you're stuck down there, Mr. Wise," Isaak laughed, his voice full of amusement. But Joffa's response was not what he expected. The giant man screamed in terror from below.

"Please, Jester, help me! I cannot stand small spaces— please, please, please!" Joffa's voice cracked, his fear evident. Isaak's amusement faltered as he realized the immense terror in Joffa's voice. The mighty warrior, reduced to a trembling wreck in a pit, was no more than a man with a crippling fear.

Isaak hesitated for a moment, but the pitiful sight tugged at something inside him. Despite the warning in his mind—and Jeremey's insistent advice—he found himself lowering a hand to the edge of the pit. "Fine, fine. Hold on," Isaak said with a sigh, and he helped Joffa out.

Once free, Joffa stood, his hands shaking as he looked at Isaak with wide, grateful eyes. "You saved me, despite all our differences and despite me trying to kill you. Why?"

Isaak shrugged, a wry grin tugging at his lips. "I suppose I just can't leave a man to his fears, no matter how big he is." He glanced at Jeremey, who merely shook his head.

Joffa, visibly moved, suddenly bowed low before Isaak, kneeling with solemn reverence. "As customary of my people, for saving me, I pledge myself to you. I will serve as your bodyguard until my dying day."

Isaak blinked in surprise, flustered by the grand gesture. He stammered, unsure of how to respond.

Rasia, on the other hand, wasted no time. She crossed her arms and glared at Joffa, her tone sharp. "First, you try to kill my love, then you pledge to protect him?" She shook her head, stepping forward to scold the now humbled Joffa. "You better remember this, Joffa. Isaak may have saved you, but don't think for one second, I'll let you off that easy."

Joffa, still kneeling, nodded vigorously, his eyes wide with a mixture of awe and fear. "I swear, Lady Rasia, I will not forget my oath."

Isaak chuckled, his embarrassment easing as Rasia's protective nature made itself known. "Well, I guess we've got a new ally then," he said with a grin, hoping Joffa wouldn't be too much trouble. Rasia, determined to ensure Isaak's contribution was acknowledged, sent a missive to the king, detailing the recapture of Castle Jezik. She carefully wrote about the battle, describing Isaak's unconventional but brave actions, playfully dubbing him the "Warrior Fool" in her letter. She also noted that some of the soldiers had begun to call him the "King of Fools," a title that, while humorous, seemed to fit his unique blend of humor and bravery. Rasia hoped the missive would help elevate Isaak's status and bring him closer to his dream.

Meanwhile, Isaak, feeling a strange sense of pride, introduced their newest member to the group—Joffa the Wise. The once-feared warrior, now humbled by his own fears, had become an unlikely ally. Isaak and Joffa sat together for a long conversation, discussing everything from battle strategies to the deeper meaning of life. To Isaak's surprise, Joffa's name was more than just an ironic title; the man was incredibly intelligent, offering insights and wisdom that Isaak had never expected from someone of his imposing size and rugged appearance. Joffa's intellect shone through as he spoke with a calm clarity, making Isaak realize that perhaps he wasn't just "Joffa the Wise" in name alone—he truly lived up to it.

As they conversed, Isaak couldn't help but feel a sense of camaraderie and respect for the man who had once been his enemy. In a way, the three of them—Rasia, Joffa, and himself—had formed an unlikely trio, each with their own strengths and quirks, but united by a shared purpose and an unexpected bond.

"Jester, you have shared with me your dream, so I feel it is only fair that I share mine with you, I wish to teach," Joffa said, his tone earnest. Isaak blinked in surprise; he had never expected this conversation to take such a turn, even after all their discussions. He leaned forward, intrigued. "And what would you teach?" he asked. Joffa's eyes lit up with enthusiasm. "I want to teach history," he replied, his voice filled with passion. "It is a subject I have always loved." Isaak listened intently as Joffa went on to explain, his words laced with nostalgia.

"Before I became a warrior, I was a scholar. History was my calling. I found the past so fascinating—each event, each story, weaving together the tapestry of our world. I excelled in it, and I always dreamed of teaching others about the lessons and knowledge of the past."

Isaak, though taken aback by the revelation, couldn't help but feel a sense of respect for the man before him.

Joffa, the once-feared warrior with a name that seemed to mock his own imposing presence, was more than just a fighter. He was a man of intellect and passion, with dreams of imparting wisdom to others. Isaak realized then that they were not so different, both driven by their desire to leave a mark on the world, albeit in very different ways.

CHAPTER SEVEN:
An audience with the King

A messenger arrived at the castle, bringing news that Isaak had earned an audience with the King and Queen. Elated, Isaak gathered Rasia, Joffa, and Jeremey, and together they made their way back to the capital. The journey was filled with excitement and nervousness; Isaak could feel the weight of the moment pressing down on him as they walked toward the royal palace. His friends offered words of encouragement, though Isaak couldn't shake the nerves building inside him.

Upon reaching the grand steps of the palace, Isaak took a deep breath, steeling himself for the moment ahead. Together, they entered the palace, where they were soon face to face with the King and Queen of Faldera. Standing beside the royal couple was the court jester, a wiry man with a sour expression, who immediately showed hostility toward Isaak. "King of Fools, bah! More like the Fool of fools!" he mocked, laughing at his own joke.

Isaak, unshaken, raised an eyebrow and responded with a grin. "I believe you have us mixed up." He then launched into a clever joke at the expense of the court jester, the room filling with laughter. The King, caught off guard by Isaak's wit, let out a hearty laugh—a sound that hadn't echoed through the palace in years. However, the Queen remained unimpressed, her gaze sharp and calculating.

"King of Fools," the King said, his tone warm with amusement. "That is quite the name you've made for yourself, Isaak." He leaned forward, intrigued. "You've certainly captured my attention. I will give you this one chance. I'm hosting a ball for my son, Prince Walter, who turns twenty-five—the same age as you, I believe." The King paused, glancing at the court jester with clear disappointment. "And I needed entertainment, which I highly doubt Urevi here can provide."

The court jester bristled at the King's words, but Isaak stood tall, his heart pounding with anticipation. This was the moment he had been waiting for.

The King leaned back on his throne, his eyes glinting with a mischievous spark. "I shall hold a contest for you two," he declared, a sly smile creeping across his face. "A contest of fools. If you win, you may become the new royal court jester. If you don't... well, you can head home. Is that a deal?"

The tension in the room thickened as the King's challenge hung in the air.

The court jester scowled, clearly displeased with the proposition, but Isaak, ever the optimist, couldn't help but grin. This was his chance.

The stakes were high, but Isaak was ready. His heart raced with excitement, and with a glance at his friends, he nodded.

"Deal," Isaak said, his voice steady and confident, despite the pressure mounting within him.

The King's smile widened. "Then let the contest of fools begin."

The King led Isaak to a lavish room, offering a place for him and his friends to rest. Isaak thanked him, then ventured out to explore the grand palace, eager to see more of the kingdom he had hoped to impress. As he wandered the hallways, he unexpectedly crossed paths with Prince Walter, a striking young man, just the same age as Isaak.

"Oh, you must be the jester who'll compete against Urevi," the prince remarked with a playful smirk. "I'm sure that won't be hard. That old fool can't even make my father laugh."

The two shared a few jokes, their laughter echoing off the marble walls. Isaak quickly realized there was more to Walter than the title of royalty suggested. The prince opened up in a way Isaak hadn't expected, revealing a side of himself that was far less guarded.

"Isaak, you are no mere jester," Walter said, his voice softening. "I can see that."

Before Isaak could respond, the prince leaned in and kissed him. Isaak caught off guard, and stepped back quickly, his heart pounding.

"I'm sorry, Your Majesty," Isaak stammered, his tone apologetic but firm. "You're a kind man, and certainly very attractive, but my heart belongs to another. I can't."

The prince's face fell, but he managed a resigned nod. "I understand," he said quietly, then hesitated before asking, "May I ask who has your heart?"

Isaak's expression softened; his eyes distant as he spoke of Rasia. "Her name is Rasia. She's strong, brave, and unlike anyone I've ever met. My heart belongs to her, and I can't imagine it being anywhere else." The passion in his words was clear, and for a moment, the two shared a quiet understanding, before Walter turned away, lost in his thoughts.

"Hm, Rasia," Prince Walter mused, a mischievous glint in his eyes. "Then she is now my rival in love. Hear me, Jester, I shall have your heart one day." The words were playful, but there was a challenge in his tone. Isaak chuckled, shaking his head.

"We'll see about that, Your Majesty," he replied, a smile tugging at his lips as the two shared a laugh.

Later, Isaak retreated to his room, focused on refining his performance for the contest. He spent the next few days with Rasia and his friends, practicing tirelessly, determined to impress not only the king but also himself.

He honed his acrobatics, his jokes, and the timing of every act, ensuring it would be a performance worthy of a royal stage.

Finally, the day arrived. It was Prince Walter's twenty-fifth birthday, and the palace was alive with the sound of music, laughter, and the bustling preparations for the grand celebration. The stage for the contest was magnificent, larger, and more elaborate than Isaak had ever seen, towering in the center of the grand hall like a challenge unto itself. The atmosphere was electric with anticipation. The contest would begin soon, and Isaak could feel the weight of the moment pressing down on him, his heart racing with both excitement and nerves.

CHAPTER EIGHT:
Contest of Fools

Isaak's heart pounded like a drum, its rhythm growing more frantic with each passing second. The sheer size of the crowd in the grand hall was overwhelming—far beyond anything he had ever faced before. His breath hitched as he tried to steady himself, but the pressure was suffocating. Unable to bear it, he slipped into a nearby empty room, his chest heaving as the walls seemed to close in around him.

A wave of panic washed over him, his hands trembling as he clutched at his mask. The room spun, a cacophony of doubts filling his mind. Then came the voice—his father's voice—a cruel echo from his past.

"You'll never make it as a royal jester, boy," the phantom words sneered.

"You're a fool, not a king."

Each phrase was a dagger, piercing his heart and shredding his confidence. Isaak sank to his knees, gripping his hatchet for comfort, trying desperately to drown out the specter of disapproval. Yet the voice only grew louder, its taunts reverberating within him, shaking the very foundation of his dream. Isaak's legs gave out beneath him, and he crumpled to the cold stone floor, his breath coming in shallow, ragged gasps. He turned his gaze upward, desperate for something to anchor him, but his eyes landed on the grand ceiling above—a mural spanning the length of the chamber. It depicted a fool in vibrant attire, dancing with exaggerated glee before a roaring crowd.

At first, it was just painting and artistry, but as Isaak stared, the image seemed to come alive. The fool twirled and leaped; his joy palpable—until the crowd turned hostile. Rotten fruit and vegetables flew from unseen hands, pelting the figure. The fool's vibrant costume dulled, his smile faded, and his dance slowed to a stumble.

Isaak's chest tightened, and his dizziness worsened. The scene unfolding above mirrored his deepest fears, feeding the spiral of doubt in his mind. His confidence, already fragile, crumbled further under the weight of the imagined ridicule. Instead of inspiration, the mural became a grim reminder of what failure might bring. As Isaak continued to watch, the mural shifted once more— this time, the fool wasn't alone. A warrior appeared, stepping out from the crowd. With tender hands, the warrior helped the fool to his feet, brushing away the remnants of the humiliation. Their connection was undeniable, and soon the two figures stood side by side, their shared strength transforming the scene into one of triumph and love.

Isaak's heart steadied, the vision igniting a warmth within him. He thought of Rasia—her fierce spirit, her unwavering belief in him, and the love they shared. The panic that gripped him began to loosen its hold. He blinked, and the mural above reverted to its original state: the fool before the crowd, frozen in painted stillness. The moving images, the story—it was all a creation of his imagination, a manifestation of his own hopes and fears.

With newfound resolve, Isaak pushed himself to his feet. He dusted off his tunic, his breath evening out as he drew in a steadying gulp of air. The memory of Rasia's smile anchored him, and with one final exhale, he prepared himself to face the performance ahead. Once Isaak steadied himself, the door creaked open, and both Rasia and Prince Walter entered, their expressions filled with concern. They paused, their eyes meeting in a moment of silent competition, before turning their attention to Isaak.

"My love, are you alright?" Rasia asked, her voice soft yet laced with worry.

"Do you need to lie down, my Jester?" Prince Walter chimed in, his tone brimming with regal care.

Isaak gave them both a reassuring smile, though he couldn't help but notice the subtle glances they exchanged—each filled with an unmistakable jealousy.

"I'm fine," Isaak replied, his voice steady. Turning toward the window, he let his gaze wander across the sprawling kingdom that stretched before the palace. His eyes found their way to the familiar outline of his village in the distance, and he felt a surge of awe and determination. It amazed him that from this vantage point, he could see the place where his dream began—and now, how close he was to achieving it.

As he stared out at the horizon, lost in thought, Rasia and Prince Walter's conversation took a more personal turn behind him. Their concern for Isaak transformed into a playful yet pointed debate about who truly held his heart.

"His heart belongs to me, prince," Rasia stated confidently, crossing her arms.

"You speak boldly, Rasia," Walter countered with a smirk. "But I assure you, his affections are far more refined than mere brute strength can claim."

Isaak chuckled softly to himself as the two continued their friendly sparring. Their words brought him comfort, reminding him of the bonds he'd formed and the love he carried with him. With one final glance at his village, he turned back to them, ready to face the challenge ahead with those he cherished by his side.

Isaak took a deep breath, brimming with newfound energy. He performed a series of practice handstands and flips, his laughter echoing through the room as he exclaimed, "I am ready!" Without hesitation, he dashed back toward the grand stage, his confidence radiating with every step.

Once onstage, Isaak clapped his hands to capture the crowd's attention and declared with exuberance, "Greetings, one and all! I am Isaak, the King of Fools! Today, I welcome you to the joyous celebration of Prince Walter's birthday." He turned toward the throne, offering a gracious bow. "And a heartfelt thanks to our noble King and Queen for granting me the honor of performing before you in this grand Contest of Fools."

He straightened, a mischievous glint in his eye. "Now, my esteemed opponent, the Royal Jester, has no opening words prepared. But fear not, for I do."

Taking another steadying breath, Isaak launched into a playful yet heartfelt poem. He began with his humble beginnings, weaving a tale of his adventures: crossing the land, battling bandits, reclaiming a castle—all delivered with clever humor and theatrical flair. The audience hung on to his every word, chuckling at his comedic takes on harrowing moments.

"And here I am now," he finished with a flourish, flipping into a one-finger handstand to display his acrobatic skill. The crowd erupted into cheers and applause.

Isaak landed gracefully and gave an exaggerated bow toward the King and Queen. "And now, let the Contest of Fools commence! May His Majesty gift us a hearty laugh and Her Majesty grace me with her signature icy glare!"

True to his words, the King burst into laughter, clapping his hands in delight. Meanwhile, the Queen regarded Isaak with her usual stern, unimpressed stare. Isaak, however, remained undaunted, meeting her gaze with a cheeky grin as the crowd cheered for what promised to be an unforgettable contest.

Isaak gave a deep, theatrical bow toward the King. "Since I am already upon this stage, my liege, may I humbly request the honor of going first?"

The King chuckled warmly, waving his hand. "Ha ha! You may, Isaak. I wish thee luck—and luck to thine opponent as well!"

The Queen, however, rolled her eyes and sighed, her voice as sharp as the winter wind. "Get on with it, fool," she said, her tone dripping with disinterest.

Unperturbed, Isaak flashed a grin and launched into his performance. He started with a series of tricks— deftly shuffling cards and juggling eggs with effortless flair—drawing cheers and gasps from the audience. With every leap and flip, he injected acrobatic prowess into the show, further fueling the crowd's excitement.

"And now," Isaak proclaimed, his voice carrying a playful lilt, "I have prepared something special for His

Majesty and the good Prince, who share a bond as legendary as the kingdom itself."

With that, Isaak executed a flawless flip off the stage, landing in front of the King with a flourish. From his pouch, he pulled two hand-carved figurines— exaggerated but unmistakable likenesses of the King and Prince Walter.

"Behold!" Isaak said, presenting the figures with a dramatic gesture. "A tribute to your legendary bond, crafted by none other than my humble hands. May these humble tokens remind all who see them of the mighty monarch and his noble heir!"

Isaak held the carved figures aloft and turned to the King and Prince with a sly smile. "Now, if Your Majesty and Your Highness would be so kind as to sign your names upon these humble creations, I shall perform a trick worthy of this grand occasion."

He handed the figurines to the King and Prince, stepping back with a flourish as they examined and signed them. Isaak waited patiently, his grin never faltering, until the signed figures were returned to him. With a playful bow, he ran back up to the stage, the figurines in hand, and turned to the audience.

"Ladies and gentlemen!" Isaak exclaimed, holding up the carved figures for all to see. "Behold the mighty King and his noble son, Prince Walter! Aren't they splendid?

See how adorable the prince looks, and how the King radiates power and grandeur!"

The crowd laughed as Isaak juggled the figurines deftly, letting them soar through the air before catching them effortlessly. He paused, holding up the two carvings for a closer look, then gasped theatrically.

"But wait!" he cried, pulling another figurine from his sleeve with an exaggerated flourish. "What is this? Could it be... our beautiful Queen?" The crowd murmured as Isaak held up the new carving—a hilariously exaggerated version of the Queen, with a sharp scowl etched across her face.

"Look at how radiant she is!" Isaak said, his voice dripping with mock admiration. "And definitely not, I repeat definitely not, brimming with malice."

The audience roared with laughter, while the Queen's icy stare intensified. Unfazed, Isaak began a series of tricks, making the figurines vanish and reappear in his hands as though by magic. He multiplied them until the stage seemed overrun with tiny carvings, only to have them vanish in a blink, leaving just the original three.

With a triumphant smile, Isaak held the figures aloft and bowed deeply to the crowd, the applause nearly deafening as the stage was set for the next part of his performance.

Isaak turned his gaze toward the youngest member of the royal family, the young Princess, who had remained quiet and observant. With a warm smile, he spoke to her directly, his tone gentle yet playful. "And is that the Princess I spy over there? Your radiance is unmistakable! I do believe I have a special gift just for you."

The Princess looked startled but intrigued as Isaak performed a series of graceful flips and twirls, seemingly from nowhere producing a small, intricately carved figurine of her likeness. In the figurine's hands was a tiny rabbit, its detail so fine that the crowd gasped in admiration. Isaak held it up for all to see.

"Now, Princess, I must ask—how did this rabbit find its way into your hands?" Isaak teased, feigning deep contemplation. "It's a mystery I simply must solve! But perhaps you can enlighten me yourself."

He motioned for the Princess to join him on the stage. She hesitated, timid and unsure, but the encouraging applause from the crowd gave her the courage to step forward. Isaak knelt to her level, speaking kindly. "Now, my dear Princess, have you ever held a rabbit before? And don't be shy—let your lovely voice carry to our splendid audience."

The Princess shook her head, her voice soft but audible, "No, I haven't."

Isaak gasped dramatically, shaking his head in mock dismay. "Well, well, then it seems my figurine has made a grave error. But wait!" He placed a colorful handkerchief over her small hands, wiggling his fingers in an exaggerated magical gesture. With a flourish, he removed the handkerchief, revealing a real, tiny rabbit—white with black spots—nestled in her palms.

The crowd erupted in astonished applause as Isaak stood and grinned. "Now, my Princess, you have held a rabbit! And this little one is my gift to you—may he bring you joy and laughter, just as you bring it to this kingdom."

He gave a deep bow, earning delighted claps from the audience. Then, with practiced precision, he tossed small, wrapped boxes toward the King, Queen, and Prince. "And for Your Majesties, I have gifts as well—inside these boxes are treasures I hope you'll cherish!"

The King laughed heartily, the Queen raised an eyebrow but accepted the gesture, and the prince smiled warmly. Isaak stood tall, the applause of the audience filling the grand hall as his performance continued to enchant all in attendance.

The King let out a booming laugh, his face lighting up with a wide grin as he examined the intricately carved figurine in his hand. "Ah, I've always wanted a likeness of myself, and with such fine craftsmanship! Truly remarkable work, Isaak," he said, turning it over in admiration.

The prince, holding his own figurine, smiled warmly. "Thank you, Isaak. I shall treasure this always," he said, pulling the jester into a brief but heartfelt hug that drew a round of affectionate murmurs from the audience.

The Queen, however, was less than impressed. She glared at the figure of herself, her lips curling in disdain. With a sharp motion, she tossed the figurine toward a nearby guard, her voice cold and cutting. "Take this away. I have no need for such trifles," she snapped, her tone dripping with displeasure. Turning her icy gaze back to Isaak, she added curtly, "Finish your act, jester. I am eager to see my fool perform."

The audience fell silent, tension thick in the air, but Isaak only smiled, bowing deeply and rising with an unshakable confidence. "Of course, Your Majesty. It seems my act must truly shine to win even a flicker of your favor," he quipped, earning a smattering of nervous laughter from the crowd. With a mischievous glint in his eye, Isaak prepared to continue, undeterred by the Queen's frosty reception.

Isaak turned to the young princess with a warm smile and gestured toward her seat. "Now, my dear princess, allow me to wish you safely back to your place of honor," he said with a bow, watching as she carefully descended the steps, clutching her newfound rabbit. Once she was seated, Isaak straightened up and addressed the audience once more.

With a flourish, he pulled out a small figurine carved in his own likeness. "Now, my esteemed friends, behold—me!" he declared, holding the tiny figure high above his head. "You may wonder why I, of all people, would have a figurine of myself. Surely, it's not because

I'm so enamored with my own reflection?" His exaggerated wink and dramatic shrug drew chuckles from the crowd.

He tossed the figurine high into the air, catching it deftly in one hand while simultaneously producing three more figurines with the other. "No, no! The reason is quite simple, you see." He held up the new figures for all to see, each exquisitely carved to represent his closest companions—his fierce and beautiful Rasia, his steadfast brother Jeremey, and the imposing yet loyal Joffa.

"These are the people who make me, me. Without them, this jester's tale would be far less colorful. Let us give them their due, for no fool is an island!" Isaak proclaimed, presenting the figurines to the audience with a dramatic bow. The crowd erupted in applause, and even the stern Queen's lips twitched, ever so slightly, as she observed his antics.

Isaak, with a mischievous grin, caught the figurine of himself mid-air and held it up for all to see. "Ah, yes! I mentioned earlier how I retook the castle, but did I ever tell you exactly how I did it?" he asked with an exaggerated tone, as if the crowd should be on the edge of their seats in suspense. With a flourish, he began to recount the moment, using his collection of figurines to act out the story. He positioned the small carvings of Rasia, Jeremey, and Joffa around him, each one taking part in the retelling with dramatic flourishes. Isaak danced, flipped, and acted with theatrical flair, bringing the battle to life in front of the royal court. His voice rose and fell with intensity, punctuating each line with a flourish of the figurines, his hands weaving an intricate dance of their own.

"And as the mighty Joffa the Wise cleaved the gates open," Isaak continued with gusto, "and Rasia, swift as the wind, dispatched our enemies..." he paused dramatically, moving the figurine of Rasia into position, "...and Jeremey, ever clever, kept the castle's treasures hidden from view, while I—" he struck a grand pose with his own figurine—"darted through the fray like a flash of lightning, reclaiming what was ours!"

The crowd laughed and cheered as Isaak ended his retelling with a dramatic flip, landing in a perfect bow. He then pulled out small balls of colored flour from his sleeve and tossed them high into the air, creating a brilliant explosion of color that cascaded down like fireworks. The vivid hues swirled in the air, mesmerizing the audience with their beauty.

Isaak, breathing heavily from his performance, stood tall and gave an exaggerated bow to the king and queen. "And as for you, my gracious queen," he said, his voice dripping with playful sarcasm, "I do hope your throne is as comfortable as it looks!"

The crowd roared with laughter, the King chuckling heartily, the prince clapping in delight, and even the Princess joining in with a light giggle. But the Queen, her face a picture of fury, slammed her fist onto the arm of her throne. "Enough of this nonsense!" she bellowed, her voice sharp and commanding. "Guards! Place this fool under arrest!"

The laughter quickly died down, the mood shifting as the guards began to move forward. Isaak, however, only gave the Queen a mock salute before spinning on his heel and darting offstage, leaving the audience in stitches and the Queen's wrath to simmer.

With a grin still plastered on his face, Isaak shrugged and called out to the crowd, "I guess that's my time, folks!" He waved to the audience, receiving a mixture of cheers and laughter in return. But before he could make his exit, the guards stepped forward, their iron chains clinking as they approached. Isaak's arms were swiftly bound, but to his surprise, the King raised a hand, halting the guards.

"Bring Isaak to me," the King commanded, his voice carrying authority. "I would not have my jester imprisoned over something as trivial as a joke—especially not one aimed at my wife." He chuckled heartily, though his eyes darted uneasily toward the Queen, who shot him a glare so sharp it could've cut glass.

Isaak, still with a playful grin, was led to stand beside the King, his chains rattling with each step. The King gave him an assuring nod. "Worry not, Isaak. I won't allow my wife to arrest you. She just needs to lighten up a bit," the King said, his voice low, though still full of humor.

Isaak let out a light laugh, but then noticed the Queen's icy glare, which seemed to freeze the very air around them. The King, unbothered by the chill, winked at Isaak and continued, "Isaak, if you ever think of getting married, remember my words—don't!" The King let out a hearty laugh, clearly amused by his own joke.

Isaak couldn't help but laugh along with the King, the tension in the room momentarily lifting. Despite his chains, Isaak felt a sense of camaraderie with the ruler, as if the weight of the situation had lessened in that brief, shared moment of humor. The Queen's glare only deepened, but the King's jovial nature seemed to soften the edges of her fury, for the moment at least.

The King, with a warm smile, placed a hand on Isaak's shoulder. "Your father must be proud of you, my boy," he said, his voice full of genuine admiration. Isaak nodded quietly, a flicker of emotion crossing his face, but he said nothing in return. The Queen, watching from the sidelines, noticed his sudden quietness, the change in his demeanor from earlier. Curiosity tugged at her, but she didn't dwell on it, dismissing it as nothing of importance.

The Royal Jester, having recovered from Isaak's performance, now made his way to the stage. With a pompous air, he gave the audience a dull, lifeless greeting.

Isaak, standing just off to the side, couldn't resist the opportunity for a little playful jab. With a sly grin, he imitated the sound of a cricket, its distinct chirp echoing through the hall. The King, alongside a few others in the crowd, burst into laughter at Isaak's impromptu joke.

The Royal Jester, his face reddening with frustration, shot a glare at Isaak, clearly irritated by the interruption. His pride, clearly bruised by the mockery, only fueled his anger. Isaak, however, continued to stand casually, a slight smile tugging at his lips, fully aware of the effect his antics had on the Royal Jester.

"I, Urevi, will not stand for this!" the Royal Jester shouted, his voice trembling with indignation. "I am better than thee! You are no king of fools; you are more of a king of stools!" His declaration hung in the air, but instead of the expected uproar of laughter, there was only a profound silence. The audience exchanged confused glances, unsure of how to respond to such an unremarkable insult.

Isaak, ever the quick wit, couldn't help himself. He called out with a grin, "Urevi, my friend, seems like no one is laughing." He offered a playful shrug, a hint of mischief dancing in his eyes. "I do wish thee luck," Isaak added with an exaggerated bow, his smile widening.

Urevi's scowl deepened, but with pride stinging his prideful heart, he proceeded with his tricks. Some worked, others failed spectacularly, yet none of them carried the same charm or finesse as Isaak's performance. The Royal Jester's act lacked the humor and lightness that had captivated the audience earlier.

From her seat, the Queen feigned amusement, forcing a small smile and clapping half-heartedly. It was a hollow display, one meant to give the illusion that she was entertained, when in truth, she couldn't be less impressed. Her forced applause was as cold as the icy glare she sent Urevi when his tricks fell flat.

The King, growing bored of Urevi's lackluster performance, turned his attention to Isaak with a more thoughtful expression. "Tell me, Isaak," King Walter began, his voice steady and curious, "why do you wish to become the royal jester?"

Isaak, sensing the sincerity in the King's inquiry, took a deep breath before launching into a heartfelt explanation. He spoke of his mother, gravely ill, and how his father worked tirelessly to support the family. "I want to bring joy and laughter to the world," Isaak continued, his eyes focused on the floor for a moment. "It's my way of making people smile, helping to ease their burdens. I thought that becoming the royal jester, serving you, would be the best way to help my family and share happiness with others."

The King listened intently, his expression softening with each word. "I see, Isaak," he said after a pause, a small but genuine smile spreading across his face. "That is quite noble of you." The King then clapped his hands together, his voice cutting through the air and halting Urevi mid-performance. The crowd fell silent, awaiting what was to come next.

"Enough of this," King Walter boomed, standing tall. "I, King Walter the First of Faldera, have made a decision. Let our fools take the stage!" His proclamation echoed throughout the room, and Isaak's heart swelled with anticipation as the spotlight shifted to him and Urevi.

The King, with a grand gesture, stood up and beckoned Isaak to join him on stage alongside Urevi. The audience hushed in anticipation, and the King began his speech, his voice carrying across the hall. "A jester," he said with authority, "is more than just a fool. A jester brings joy, laughter, and unity to the people. They remind us that even in the hardest of times, a smile can heal."

He paused for dramatic effect, then continued, "And now, I give the honor of royal jester to... Isaak, the King of Fools!"

A burst of laughter and applause followed as the King placed a regal jester's hat atop Isaak's head. Isaak could hardly contain his excitement. With a few quick twirls and flips, he let out a joyful cheer. "Thank you, Your Highness! I appreciate this more than you would ever know!" Isaak's voice rang with gratitude and joy as he bowed deeply to the audience.

Without a moment's hesitation, Isaak rushed toward Rasia, who stood in the crowd. He kissed her with a passion that spoke volumes of his love, and the crowd cheered at the sight of their affection.

The King, smiling warmly at the scene, approached them. "Ah, young love," he mused with a wink, his gaze shifting to Isaak. "Your heart is as full as your talent. You've earned this."

Then, with a gesture of kindness and generosity, the King spoke again. "Isaak, I believe family is everything. Your family is welcome to live here at the palace. Bring them to us; they shall find a home with me."

Overwhelmed with joy, Isaak's eyes sparkled as he hugged the King tightly. "Thank you, Your Majesty! You have no idea what this means to me!"

Isaak dashed from the stage, his heart pounding with happiness as he ran to his room. There, he began to pack, his mind racing with excitement. He would finally bring his family to the palace—a dream he had never dared to believe could come true. Isaak finished packing his belongings, the weight of his excitement evident in every step as he walked out of his room. With his bag slung over his shoulder and walking stick in hand, he met the King and Queen just outside. Their children were with them, standing proudly by their sides.

"Your Highnesses," Isaak greeted with a deep bow, a show of the utmost respect.

"I'm off to bring my family, just as you suggested, my King," he added, a note of gratitude in his voice.

The King smiled warmly; his eyes filled with wisdom. "May your journey be safe, Isaak. Remember, the greatest treasures lie not in wealth or glory, but in the people who walk beside you. Family is the true joy of life."

The Queen, though less enthusiastic, offered a half-hearted congratulations. "Safe travels, Jester. "Don't be gone too long," she said, her tone cool but polite.

The Prince and Princess, however, were more animated in their farewell. The Princess rushed forward and gave Isaak a hug. "Jester, when you return, we must have tea together. I'll bring Zigbar!" she said with a bright smile.

Isaak raised an eyebrow, intrigued. "Zigbar, you say? And who might that be?"

The Princess giggled, her eyes sparkling. "It's the rabbit you gave me, silly! I named him Zigbar."

Isaak laughed heartily; his spirits lifted by her joy. "Zigbar, then. I look forward to meeting him. And I will certainly join you for tea."

The prince let out a hearty laugh and then quickly apologized for his sister's antics. "No need to apologize for her, My Prince," Isaak replied with a grin, brushing off any concern. The two shared a small conversation, the air light and easy between them.

"Be safe, my Jester. Come back unharmed," the prince said sincerely, pulling Isaak into a deep hug.

The Queen, however, scowled at the display, her patience running thin. "That's enough, son. Please, don't hug the fool. Who knows where he's been?" she remarked, her voice laced with disdain.

Isaak, ever quick with a joke, retorted with a smirk, "Oh, I know where I've been, but do you know where you've been?"

With a mischievous laugh, Isaak dashed away, his voice echoing through the halls as he made his way back to the King's road. His heart was light, filled with excitement for the journey ahead. Behind him, Rasia, Jeremey, and Joffa followed closely, ready to begin this new chapter of their adventure together.

CHAPTER NINE:
No comedy without tragedy

Isaak and his companions paused for a well-earned break just outside the capital, their spirits high from the excitement of the recent celebration. They sat together, reflecting on the contest and how Isaak had triumphed over the royal jester.

"I'm excited to go home and bring my family to the palace," Isaak said with a smile. "They'll be so proud of me. And having all of you by my side fills my heart with a joy I can't explain."

Joffa grinned and gave a nod of approval. "My friend, though I've known you for only a short while, I can say this—you're a good man. To be accepted by you is truly an honor."

Jeremey, always the thoughtful one, added a few words of appreciation as well, grateful for their journey together.

Rasia, ever affectionate, held Isaak close, her words soft and sincere. "Oh, my funny Jester, how I love thee. If anyone dares to attack you, they shall not live to regret it, for I will be there, always by your side."

Isaak's heart swelled with love and gratitude for his friends and Rasia, knowing that no matter what lay ahead, they would face it together. Isaak let out a nervous chuckle, feeling the weight of the love surrounding him, a warmth that filled his heart—and, to his surprise, a flutter of arousal for Rasia. Her strength, both physical and emotional, always had a way of lifting him up, giving him a boost of energy. He couldn't help but admire her, knowing she was always there for him.

The group continued their journey home, sharing stories and laughter along the way, the road feeling less long with friends by his side. They made a stop at a village near Isaak's hometown, where Isaak, always eager to perform, set up to entertain the crowd. The villagers were excited to see him, their cheers and applause making Isaak feel like a true star. Everyone knew him here, and their enthusiasm was infectious.

However, there was one person in the crowd who wasn't clapping, who wasn't cheering—Urevi, the old jester. Isaak spotted him almost immediately, standing in the back with a scowl. Urevi's voice rang out, mocking Isaak with harsh words. But Isaak was quick-witted as ever, firing back with quips and jokes that had the crowd laughing and Urevi's attempts to spoil the fun falling flat.

With each jab from Urevi, Isaak only grew more confident, his performance turning into a dance of words and wit. Urevi's heckling didn't faze him—if anything, it fueled his energy, and the audience was loving every moment of it.

Isaak, always quick with a prank, saw an opportunity to get back at Urevi for his heckling. With a sly grin, he sprayed colorful water into Urevi's eyes, then performed an acrobatic flip for added flair. The crowd laughed, unaware of the tragic turn that would follow.

But as Urevi stumbled, blinded by the spray, he lost his balance and fell off the stage. Isaak watched in horror as Urevi collided with a jagged piece of broken wood that pierced his chest. Time seemed to freeze as Urevi's lifeless body crumpled to the ground, and the laughter of the crowd died instantly. A heavy silence hung in the air, the realization of what had just happened crashing over Isaak like a wave.

Isaak stood frozen; disbelief etched on his face. He didn't know what to do, his hands trembling, his heart racing in panic. The crowd, too, was still unsure of what to say or do in the wake of the accident. Without a word, Isaak turned and fled, his friends running alongside him as they made their way back to his village.

But just before they reached the gates, Isaak collapsed to his knees, tears streaming down his face. The weight of the moment was too much for him to bear, and his body shook with the force of his grief. Rasia knelt beside him, her hand on his shoulder, trying to comfort him, but Isaak could barely speak through the sobs.

"I...I killed a man," he whispered, his voice breaking with the enormity of his words.

Rasia, though worried, gently tried to console him. "It wasn't your fault, Isaak," she said softly, but Isaak couldn't stop crying.

"No, you don't understand, my love," he managed, his breath coming in ragged gasps. "I've killed brigands, men with evil hearts, those who wished harm upon me. But that man... he was innocent. I killed an innocent man."

His voice quivered with guilt, the burden of the mistake weighing heavily on his soul. His friends exchanged worried glances, but no words could take away the ache that Isaak felt deep within. Isaak's mind spiraled further as he looked down at his hands, now seeming stained with the blood of the man he had unintentionally killed. His gaze fixed on them, horror evident in his eyes as he whispered, "How can I look upon my family while my hands are stained with the blood of my fellow man? Not just any man, but a man who was like me, a jester, and innocent."

His heart pounded in his chest, a cold sweat running down his face as he believed the blood to be real. Desperate, he took a piece of cloth from his bag and began rubbing his hands frantically, trying to erase the imagined blood. His movements were erratic, wild with panic as he furiously scrubbed, convinced the blood would never come off.

But as he continued, Rasia, Jeremey, and Joffa watched in growing concern, their eyes flicking from Isaak to his hands. To them, there was no blood. Isaak's hands were clean, as spotless as they had been before. Yet Isaak, lost in his grief and guilt, saw only the dark red stains that weren't there.

His actions only made his friends more worried. "Isaak, there's nothing there," Rasia said gently, reaching out to take his hands. "You're not stained. You didn't kill him intentionally."

But Isaak could not hear her. His mind was consumed by the illusion of blood, his emotions overwhelming him. His hands were shaking, his breath quick and shallow. "I have to get it off... it won't come off!" he cried, continuing to rub at his hands with the cloth.

Joffa stepped closer, placing a hand on Isaak's shoulder. "Isaak, please... There's nothing on your hands. You didn't do this on purpose," he tried to reassure him, but the words barely seemed to penetrate Isaak's panic.

Isaak, still trapped in his own mind, couldn't let go of the belief that he was tainted. The worry from his friends only deepened, but no amount of reassurance could calm Isaak's frantic mind in that moment. Joffa's voice was gentle, yet firm as he said, "My friend, please stop. You'll hurt yourself." He quickly reached out and grabbed Isaak's hands, halting the frantic rubbing. Isaak didn't respond, his eyes glassy with panic, his mind replaying the horrific moment of Urevi's death over and over again. The image of the man falling, the deadly accident, consumed him.

Joffa, seeing Isaak's distress, took a deep breath before speaking again, trying to offer some wisdom to calm his friend. "Isaak, my friend, you are not the cause of this. What happened was an accident. You didn't mean to hurt him." But Isaak didn't hear him. His thoughts were too loud, his guilt too overwhelming.

"How can I talk to my mother?" Isaak whispered, his voice shaky with fear and grief. "Look upon these hands of mine, Joffa. They no longer spread joy but tragedy." Isaak held out his hands, as if showing them to Joffa for the first time, the cloth still clutched in his grip.

Joffa and Jeremey exchanged worried glances, but Joffa responded first, his voice steady but full of compassion. "Isaak, your family will love you no matter what, just like we do. You are not defined by one moment of tragedy."

Rasia, ever by his side, stepped forward and placed a hand on his shoulder, her words soft but firm. "You are loved, Isaak. You are more than just a moment. Don't carry this guilt alone."

Isaak's lips trembled as he gave a small, shaky smile, the words soothing him just enough for the moment. But the pain in his heart was still raw, and the fear in his eyes remained.

Still, he stood up, wiping away the remnants of his emotional outburst. He reached for his mask, the familiar weight of it giving him some semblance of control. He knew the mask was a shield, a way to hide his vulnerability, even if only for a while.

Walking toward the gate, Isaak caught sight of old Henry, a familiar face. Henry greeted him with a warm, comforting hug, his arms a reminder of home. Isaak hesitated for a moment, then allowed himself to lean into the embrace, the weight of his burdens slightly lighter in the presence of someone who cared for him.

Henry's voice was warm and welcoming as he greeted Isaak, "My friend, you've returned. Does thou have good tidings? Tell me, did you achieve the dream?" Isaak took a deep breath before recounting everything that had transpired. He told Henry of his victory at the palace, his new title as royal jester, and the joy he felt in bringing his friends along for the journey. He introduced Joffa, Jeremey, and Rasia, all of whom had become integral parts of his life, though he carefully omitted the tragic incident with Urevi. That was something too painful, too raw, to speak of just yet.

Henry listened attentively, a proud smile tugging at the corners of his lips. But as Isaak finished, the older man's expression shifted, and a shadow of sorrow passed over his face. "How are my family, Sirrah Henry?" Isaak asked, eager to hear of his mother's health and the state of his household.

Henry's smile faltered, his voice growing softer as he replied, "They are home, waiting for thee." He paused, his eyes glistening with a mix of concern and something more sorrowful. "And I'm sorry."

The words hung heavily in the air, their weight settling on Isaak's chest. He didn't fully understand, but the look in Henry's eyes told him that something wasn't right. The smile that had once been so genuine had faded into something more guarded.

Isaak, though confused and unsettled by Henry's cryptic words, didn't dwell on them. His heart was set on seeing his mother again, on feeling the comfort of his family after so long. With a nod, he gave his friends a brief smile and set off toward his family home, his anticipation growing with each step, eager to finally return to the place he had longed for since his departure. The moment he'd been waiting for was just within reach—seeing his mother, feeling her embrace, and sharing the joy of his success with her.

Isaak arrived home, his small cottage looking smaller than he remembered, but still filled him with a warmth that he had missed deeply. He smiled softly as he looked at the familiar, humble structure. "This is my home," he said to his friends, his voice a mix of nostalgia and pride. "It may not be the palace, but it is home." His words carried a deep affection for the place that had once been his world.

As Isaak and his group entered, he was immediately greeted by his sister, and they shared a joyful reunion. Isaak enveloped her in a deep, heartfelt hug, grateful to be in her presence once more. "Oh, Isaak, I'm so glad you returned," she said, her voice trembling slightly with emotion. "We all have missed you so much, but there's something I must tell you."

Before she could continue, Isaak beamed and introduced his friends, starting with Rasia. "And this," Isaak said with a tender smile, "is the love of my life, Rasia."

Rasia, ever graceful, bowed before Isaak's sister, then embraced her in a bear hug, showing the warmth and kindness she had already displayed to Isaak's closest friends. His sister laughed, her joy infectious, as she welcomed Rasia into the fold with open arms.

The moment was filled with love, laughter, and a sense of homecoming that Isaak had longed for, the weight of past struggles melting away in the comfort of his family and the presence of his beloved Rasia. He stood, surrounded by those he held dear, knowing that despite the challenges ahead, he had everything he needed right here—love, family, and the promise of a future filled with laughter.

"It is an honor to meet you, Wina. Isaak told me so much of thee," Rasia said warmly, offering a polite smile.

Wina, who had been quietly observing Isaak's friends with a reserved expression, smiled back. "Thank you," she replied graciously, though her voice was tinged with concern. "But I must speak with Isaak."

She turned, her gaze searching for him, but Isaak was nowhere in sight. Confused, Wina looked around, only to find that Isaak had already made his way to his mother's room.

Inside, Isaak was kneeling beside his mother's bed, her condition worse than when he had left. The sight of her frailty struck him with a pang of guilt and sorrow. He had longed for this moment to return to her, to share the good news, but now, his heart ached as he saw her struggling.

"Mama, I am home," Isaak whispered softly as he ran to her side, sliding to kneel beside the bed. His hands gently took hers, his thumb stroking her fragile skin. "Your little jester is home, and I bring good tidings."

He explained everything—the contest he had won, the journey he had undertaken, the friends he had made, and the love he had found in Rasia. His words filled the room with a sense of warmth, a slight comfort for the woman who had suffered for so long. He spoke with enthusiasm, joy, and hope for their future together, but he omitted the darker part of his journey—the death of Urevi, the man he had accidentally killed. He couldn't bring himself to mention it, not now, not in front of his mother.

As Isaak spoke, he held her hand tighter, hoping that his return, his good fortune, would bring some peace to her ailing heart. His mind, however, remained heavy with the burden he had yet to share.

"Oh my. My little king of fools, I am so glad you are home. If only your father were still here," Isaak's mother said with a tender smile, but the words hung heavily in the air, their weight pressing down on Isaak's chest.

The mention of his father sent a shock through Isaak, and his heart skipped a beat. "Father? What do you mean? Is he not here?" Isaak asked, his voice laced with confusion and a hint of dread.

Yenn's smile faded almost immediately, and her eyes filled with a deep sadness. She looked away for a moment, as if gathering the strength to speak. The room, once filled with the warmth of reunion, now felt colder, heavier.

"He... he passed away while you were gone," she whispered, her voice trembling. "It was sudden. I didn't want to burden you with it before, but now that you're home, I thought you should know."

Isaak's world seemed to tilt, the ground beneath him unstable. His mind raced, struggling to comprehend the news. His father, the man who had been the pillar of his life, the one who had always supported him, was gone.

"Father..." Isaak repeated, his voice hoarse. He had never expected this, never imagined he would return to a world where his father was no longer there. It felt like a cruel twist of fate, to come home triumphant and full of hope only to be met with the loss of the one person who he had always wanted to impress.

Yenn reached out, her frail hand gently resting on Isaak's, offering what little comfort she could. But Isaak, lost in the shock of the moment, barely registered the touch. The grief, sudden and overwhelming, wrapped around him like a cloak, leaving him speechless.

Isaak trembled as he whispered, "How... how did he die?" His voice barely above a whisper, the weight of his grief pressing down on him.

Yenn, with a gentle squeeze of his hand, took a deep breath before answering, her voice soft and filled with sorrow. "He died from exhaustion... He overworked himself, trying so hard to provide, wanting you to come home to a happy family. When he heard news of your exploits, it never failed to make him smile. He was proud of you, Isaak. I have no doubt about that. He would come into my room, reading your letters, and we would both be so proud. He would be proud of you if he were able to say so."

Isaak stood in silence, his heart aching at the thought of his father, gone too soon, his love for Isaak never unspoken but unexpressed in the end. He leaned down and kissed his mother on the cheek, a silent promise to carry forward the pride his father had left behind.

Without a word, Isaak began gathering his mother's things, the action mechanical, a way for him to focus his grief on something tangible. He packed the few belongings she had in her small room, his movements slow and deliberate, each item a reminder of a life once shared.

Yenn watched him, her expression a mixture of sadness and understanding. "What are you doing, dear?" she asked softly, her voice tinged with worry.

Isaak, not looking up from his task, replied with quiet determination, "I'm packing your things, mama. We are going to the palace."

The words were final, a promise to his mother, to his father's memory. Isaak wasn't just returning to the palace for himself; he was bringing his family with him, honoring his father's wish for a better life. The palace would be a place for them now, a place where they could be safe, where Isaak could finally give them the life his father had hoped for.

Isaak retreated to his room; his mind heavy with questions he didn't want to ask but couldn't stop pondering. He stood in front of the mirror, his reflection grimy and worn, a physical reflection of the turmoil within him. His eyes traced the person staring back at him—was he truly the jester he had always dreamed of becoming? Was he living up to what his father had envisioned for him?

His mind drifted back to a memory, one from when he was just a child, no older than four. It was a beautiful night, the sky painted with stars. Isaak had been sitting on his father's lap, looking up at him with innocent wonder.

"What is a jester, papa?" Isaak had asked, his voice full of curiosity.

His father smiled warmly, his eyes kind with wisdom. "A jester brings joy to others, Isaak. When I was your age, I saw a jester perform, and the joy he brought to the crowd was a wondrous sight. A jester is someone who can make others smile, laugh, and forget their worries, even for just a little while."

Isaak's heart ached as he brought himself back to the present. Standing before the same mirror, his gaze now hardened with regret and grief, he whispered, "Did I live up to your expectations, papa? I came home, papa. Why did you have to work so hard?"

Tears welled up in Isaak's eyes, the weight of his emotions finally breaking free. His hand clenched into a fist, the pain of his father's death, the guilt of not being enough, and the pressure of trying to be something he was not, all collided. He punched the mirror, the glass shattering on impact, the sharp edges slicing into his hand. Blood pooled from the cuts, staining his skin, but

Isaak didn't care. The pain was momentary, compared to the ache in his chest.

His hands, now trembling with the blood and broken glass, were a grim reminder of the darkness he had been trying to outrun. He looked at the shards that lay scattered on the floor, each piece a distorted reflection of himself. Rasia rushed in, alarmed by the sound of glass shattering. When she saw Isaak on the floor, blood staining his hand as tears streamed down his face, her heart broke. Without a second thought, she knelt beside him, pulling him into her arms, offering the comfort he so desperately needed.

"Shhh, shed no more tears, my love," she whispered softly, her voice soothing as she gently cradled him. She carefully took his hand in hers; her fingers tender as she picked the shards of glass from his bleeding palm. "I am here."

Isaak, overwhelmed by the grief and guilt weighing on him, let out a shaky breath, his tears soaking into Rasia's shoulder. She worked silently, her touch gentle, cleaning and bandaging his wounds. As she finished, she sat beside him, holding him close, giving him the time he needed to compose himself.

After a long silence, Isaak wiped his eyes and spoke, his voice thick with emotion. "My father... he used to laugh with me. He'd get so angry sometimes, but he'd still make me laugh."

Rasia smiled softly, sensing the weight of the memory. Isaak continued, his voice growing steadier as he recalled one of his father's more colorful moments.

"One time he got so angry at me for pranking the village elder," Isaak said, his lips curling into a slight smile. "He gave me quite the yell, one that the entire village could hear. It was so loud; I think even the cows stopped grazing."

Rasia chuckled at the image, her fingers gently brushing through his hair, helping him find a moment of peace amidst the storm of emotions. Isaak laughed softly too, the memory of his father's stern but loving nature a brief comfort in the midst of his grief. They sat there for a moment, the quiet conversation giving Isaak a small sense of relief, even as the weight of the past lingered on his heart.

Isaak gently held Rasia's hand, guiding her out of the house and toward his special place—the large tree that had always been his sanctuary. "This is where I come to think... to dream," he said, his voice soft with reverence as they approached the towering tree. Rasia marveled at its size, the branches reaching up to the sky as if they were ancient and full of stories.

She squeezed his hand gently, moved by the peacefulness of the place. "It's beautiful, Isaak."

Isaak smiled, a playful glint in his eyes. "This is also where my best jokes are made." He laughed, leading her to the base of the tree. They sat beneath it, Isaak holding Rasia close as the day began to fade, the warmth of the sun giving way to the cool evening air.

As the last of the sunlight slipped away, the moonlight began to fill the space around them, casting a soft, ethereal glow. Isaak looked up at the sky and then back at Rasia, a smile forming on his lips. "This is the part I love most of all, my dear. Watch closely."

Rasia followed his gaze, and slowly, one by one, dozens of fireflies appeared, their tiny lights flickering like stars coming to life. The sky was soon filled with their soft glow, a magical dance of light in the air around them. Isaak's eyes sparkled as he watched her reaction, his heart swelling with the beauty of the moment.

"Do you see, Rasia?" he whispered. "This is magic. Not the kind that comes from tricks or jokes, but the kind that's just... pure and beautiful."

Rasia smiled, her eyes shining as she nestled closer to him, the glow of the fireflies lighting up their faces. "I see it, Isaak. It's perfect."

They sat in silence, surrounded by the gentle flicker of the fireflies, the world around them quiet and serene, as if even time itself had paused to take in the beauty of that moment. As the night unfolded, Isaak and Rasia lay beneath the stars, the vast sky above them stretching endlessly. Isaak's worries and fears, which had clung to him for so long, seemed to drift away in the comfort of

Rasia's arms. Her soft, steady breathing lulled him into a peaceful rest.

"I love you, Rasia," Isaak whispered, the words carrying a weight of sincerity and warmth.

Rasia, nestled beside him, smiled softly, the only answer the gentle rise and fall of her chest as she slept peacefully.

Hours passed, and as the night slowly gave way to the first light of dawn, the two awoke. The soft golden light of the morning filtered through the leaves above them. Rasia sat up, brushing the sleep from her eyes and stretching as she rose to her feet.

She turned to Isaak, her eyes full of tenderness. "I'll head on back without you," she said gently. "I wish to stay here just a few minutes longer," Isaak replied, his voice calm, as he remained seated beneath the tree.

Rasia gave him a soft smile, understanding, and with a last lingering look at Isaak, she began to head back toward the village, leaving Isaak with his thoughts and the quiet peace of the morning.

Isaak sat there, his back against the tree, the world around him still and quiet. The weight of the previous days seemed lighter now, and as the sun continued to rise, he took a deep breath, allowing the serenity of the moment to settle over him.

Rasia, with a quiet nod, turned to continue packing the rest of Isaak's belongings. She moved swiftly, helping Isaak's mother onto a carriage, ensuring everything was in order for their journey. Isaak, however, remained under the large tree, his thoughts consumed with the weight of everything that had transpired. The tragedy that had befallen him—the murder, the guilt, the loss of his father—crushed him like a heavy stone.

He sat for a while, lost in the stillness of the morning, before finally standing up, putting on his mask to hide the turmoil within. With a deep breath, he walked toward the carriage, his voice ringing out with a forced cheer. "Now onto the royal palace, family," he exclaimed, his words carrying a sense of finality and determination, though his heart remained heavy.

As they left the village behind, Isaak took one last look at the life he had known, a bittersweet farewell to the familiar sights and sounds of home. They passed by Henry's small cottage, where the old man stood waiting. Henry gave Isaak a heartfelt goodbye, his eyes filled with emotion. Isaak, struggling to mask his own sorrow, walked over and embraced him, murmuring a quiet "Thank you" before stepping into the carriage.

With a final wave, the family left the village, the dust of the road rising behind them as they ventured toward the royal palace, a new chapter in Isaak's life awaiting them.

Isaak, along with his friends and family, made their way toward the capital. They traveled slowly, making occasional stops at other villages, though they carefully avoided the one where Isaak had accidentally caused a man's death. Along the way, Isaak kept his sister and mother entertained, sharing tales of his adventures. Some of the stories were humorous, others filled with the excitement of his travels, but each one brought a lightness to their hearts during the long journey.

Before long, they arrived at the capital. Isaak was met by familiar guards, who greeted him with warmth and enthusiasm. "Welcome back, Isaak! The royal family awaits your return!" they said, their voices full of genuine joy.

As they approached the royal palace, Isaak helped his mother off the carriage, supporting her as they made their way inside. He introduced his family to the King and Queen, who welcomed them with open arms. The Queen, though still stern in many ways, had softened her demeanor. Seeing Isaak's mother in such a fragile state, she led her to a comfortable room, ensuring that the best medical care was available to her.

Isaak's heart swelled with gratitude as he watched his family be taken care of. It was clear that, despite the burdens he carried, there was a sense of relief in finally being home. The palace's grandeur, the warmth of the royal family, and the care his mother received all made

Isaak feel like his dreams were slowly coming true, though a shadow of sorrow still lingered in his heart.

Isaak's heart felt heavy as the King asked, "And where is your father, the one you spoke of? I do not see him." With a deep breath, Isaak explained, his voice faltering, how his father had passed away from exhaustion, working tirelessly in the hopes that Isaak would return home to a happy family. Isaak couldn't help but feel a pang of guilt as he recalled how he hadn't been there when his father had needed him most.

"I'm sorry, my boy," the King said softly, his eyes filled with empathy. "I'm sure he was a great man, and he would be proud of you." The King gave Isaak a solemn smile, his words offering some small comfort. He then escorted Isaak back to the royal jester's quarters, his voice full of kindness. "Sleep well, my boy. Your family is in good hands, and it was a delight to meet your mother and sister."

As Isaak stood at the doorway of his quarters, he turned to see the Queen approaching. Her face, usually stern and unyielding, was softened by sympathy. "I know that you know I don't like you," she said quietly, "but I am sorry you lost your father." Isaak, surprised by her rare show of kindness, nodded slowly, feeling the weight of her words sink in.

The Queen, after offering her condolences, left the room and made her way to a private chamber, where she met with Aleksi, the head of the kingdom's spy network. "Aleksi," she said in a hushed tone, "I want you to gather any information you can about the new jester. And do keep an eye on him." Her words were filled with an air of caution as she gave her orders. After their conversation, she went to her own room, where the King was waiting for her.

Meanwhile, Isaak stood in his new room, his eyes drawn to the clean mirror before him. "Another mirror for me to look upon the sham that I am," he muttered under his breath, the weight of his self-doubt pressing down on him. As he unpacked, he carefully placed a child's painting of his father on his desk. It had once been a gift, a token of his young love and admiration for the man who had worked so tirelessly for their family. Now, it was a memento of loss, a reminder of the father he had failed to protect, and the man he had hoped to live up to.

Isaak ran his fingers gently over the edges of the painting, his heart heavy with regret, but also with a quiet resolve to make his father proud, even if it was too late to do so in life. Unable to keep still, Isaak wandered through the grand halls of the palace, his mind restless. As he roamed, he found himself drawn to the ballroom, its opulent design almost calling to him. The room was empty, save for his imagination, which quickly filled the space with visions of a wondrous celebration. In his mind, the ballroom was alive with swirling dancers, guests in elegant attire, and the royal family in the midst of a joyous gathering. Laughter and conversation echoed as the finest of banquets were spread across the tables, each dish more luxurious than the last.

As Isaak's feet moved seemingly of their own accord, he imagined himself swept into a dance. Rasia appeared in his arms; her smile radiant as they waltzed across the polished floor. Isaak's jokes flowed easily, each one earning a bright laugh from Rasia as they moved gracefully together. They gazed into each other's eyes, lost in the shared joy of the moment. For a brief instant, the weight of his troubles seemed to vanish, replaced by a fleeting sense of happiness and peace.

But the moment was shattered when the voice of the prince echoed through the room, breaking Isaak from his reverie. "Why are you dancing alone, my Jester?" he called out, his tone full of curiosity.

Isaak chuckled softly, still a bit disoriented from his daydream. "Oh, I'm just daydreaming, Your Majesty," he replied with a lighthearted smile, though inside, a part of him longed for the dance to have been real.

The prince laughed heartily, a playful glint in his eyes. "Well, dream on, my friend. But allow me this dance," he said, extending his hand to Isaak.

Isaak hesitated for a moment, then took the prince's hand, his curiosity piqued. The prince guided him into position, and together they began to waltz across the ballroom. "One, two, three, and one..." Isaak whispered to himself, trying to match the prince's movements. His soft repetition made the prince laugh.

"Now, Isaak," the prince said as they twirled, "I know I am not the one you love, but I do hope we can be friends?" Isaak smiled, touched by the sincerity in the prince's words. "Of course, Your Highness, I would be honored."

Isaak couldn't help but tease lightly, "Rasia would be glad that you are no longer her competition." The prince raised an eyebrow but replied with a grin, "Oh, don't get me wrong, my jester. I don't plan on giving up anytime soon."

Isaak blushed at the prince's playful confidence, and the prince burst into laughter, thoroughly enjoying the lighthearted exchange. The two continued to dance, the air filled with a surprising sense of camaraderie, their playful banter blending with the graceful rhythm of their steps.

The prince chuckled and said, "Now Isaak, my sister wishes to see you again. She has been waiting eagerly for a tea party with you."

Isaak immediately stopped dancing and performed a dramatic bow. "Of course, Your Majesty! I too have longed for a tea party," he said in a playful tone. With that, he skipped away, heading toward the princess's chambers.

As Isaak entered, the princess greeted him with a warm hug. "Isaak, you're back! I'm so glad to see you, and so is Zigbar—look at him hop around!" She pointed excitedly at her rabbit, which was happily bouncing around the room.

Isaak smiled and grinned at her enthusiasm. "Of course I came back, Princess! And I brought a friend of my own—my best friend." He then whistled, and soon, his pet pig, Lawrance, trotted into the room, giving cheerful oinks as he waddled over to the princess. Isaak then pulled out a small jester hat from his pocket and placed it carefully on Lawrance's head. "Behold, Princess, this is my best friend, Lawrance," Isaak announced proudly. "Give a bow, Lawrance, she is royalty."

Lawrance, ever the obedient pig, lowered his head in what looked like a respectful bow, letting out a soft oink. The princess couldn't contain her laughter, giggling at the sight. She gave a playful curtsy in return. "Welcome, Sir Lawrance," she said with a smile, bowing to the pig as if he were a true noble.

She gently petted Lawrance, who seemed to enjoy the attention. Isaak, delighted by the interaction, set up a small tea party for the four of them. Isaak, in his usual theatrical way, sipped imaginary tea from an empty cup, while feeding Lawrance a crunchy carrot. The princess laughed at every joke Isaak made, the room filled with lighthearted chatter and joy.

The tea party was simple, yet filled with warmth and happiness,

Isaak finished his imaginary tea, gave the princess a dramatic curtsy, and then left the room with Lawrance trotting happily behind him. The two made their way back to Isaak's room, where he collapsed onto the bed, feeling the weight of the day's events. He sighed deeply, exhausted from the whirlwind of activities, conversations, and performances.

Rasia, having followed him quietly, entered the room and climbed onto the bed beside him. She nestled close, wrapping her arms around Isaak as he did the same. They held each other in a comfortable silence, both expressing the exhaustion of the day in their own way. The world outside seemed to fade as they lay there, finding solace in each other's presence, letting the tiredness wash over them together.

In the peacefulness of their shared moment, Isaak's thoughts slowed, and for the first time in a long while, he simply allowed himself to rest. Later that night, after the royal household had fallen into a deep sleep, the queen crept into a private chamber, her footsteps soft and deliberate. She met with Aleksi, her trusted spymaster. As she entered, a devilish smile curved her lips, and her eyes gleamed with anticipation.

"So, do you have news for me, Aleksi?" she asked in a low voice, clearly eager for any information that could give her the upper hand.

Aleksi, with his grizzled voice that sounded like gravel being ground, replied cautiously, his tone hushed. "Well, my queen, seems like most love him. Not many have something bad to say, but I have found a few things."

The queen's smile widened, a glimmer of excitement in her eyes. This unnerved Aleksi, who shifted uncomfortably, but he continued.

"Good," she said, leaning in slightly. "Tell me then, Aleksi. What have you learned?"

Aleksi hesitated for a moment; his face clouded with doubt. "Does the king know you asked me this?"

At the mention of her husband, the queen's smile faltered for just a second, replaced by a sharp frown. "The king needn't know everything, my old friend," she replied coldly. "Now, tell me everything you've learned." Aleksi swallowed nervously before continuing. "Of course, my queen," he began, his voice low and hesitant. "Well, to start, it seems our Jester has a history. He's been caught stealing on a few occasions, not just once but multiple times. Not only that, but before he came to the palace, he had quite the reputation for being... debaucherous." He paused, gauging the queen's reaction, but she remained silent, her gaze sharp and focused on him.

"But" Aleksi continued, his voice dropping even lower, "the biggest news is far darker. He's a murderer... and a recent one." The queen raised an eyebrow, her curiosity piqued.

Aleksi then recounted the incident, explaining how Isaak had accidentally killed the old jester during a performance. The queen listened intently, her smile slowly returning as she processed the information.

"Oh, my," she said, her voice dripping with satisfaction. "Now that is good."

The queen's eyes glinted with cold determination as she formulated her plan. "Aleksi," she began in a mocking tone, "once morning comes, I want you to grab our dear new jester." She smirked, the cruel edge of her words unmistakable. "And once you do, I want you to interrogate him. Get him to confess, and then, I want him hanged at dawn the day after." Her tone shifted to one of menace as she laid out her orders.

Aleksi's heart sank at the thought, but he knew better than to refuse. He swallowed his discomfort and nodded reluctantly. "Of course, my queen," he replied before turning and leaving the room. The queen, satisfied with the plan, returned to her quarters, where the king sat up in bed, his voice filled with concern. "Where did you go, my dear?" he asked, his gaze fixed on her as she entered the room. The queen replied with a practiced smile, her voice casual as she said,

"Oh, just on a nightly stroll to help me sleep." She yawned dramatically, slipping into the bed beside her husband. She whispered a soft goodnight to him, watching as he drifted off to sleep just moments later, unaware of the plans she had set in motion.

CHAPTER TEN:
Taken

The morning light slowly crept into the cold, dark dungeon, stirring Isaak from his slumber. His eyes snapped open to find himself chained to a chair, the cold stone walls around him pressing in. In front of him stood Aleksi, holding a burning rod.

"What's going on? Who are you?" Isaak gasped, his heart pounding in his chest.

Aleksi's voice was calm, almost sympathetic. "I'm sorry, my friend, but my orders are orders." He then swung the hot rod and smacked Isaak's leg, making him cry out in pain.

Isaak's eyes widened in horror. "Why?!" he screamed in fear, the pain searing through him.

Aleksi sighed, his face hardening. "She just doesn't like you; I believe. Other than that, you murdered a man... she wants you to confess."

Isaak's heart sank as the memory of the accidental death flooded his mind, playing out once again, just like the haunting vision of the mural. His breath quickened, and for a moment, everything seemed to blur around him.

In a hushed tone, Isaak finally spoke, his voice trembling. "It was an accident. I didn't mean to."

But even as the words left his lips, he didn't believe them. Deep down, a nagging feeling gripped his chest. It wasn't just an accident—something inside him whispered that it was his fault. The weight of guilt pressed heavily on his heart, and he felt like he was drowning in it.

Aleksi's gaze remained cold and calculating as he looked at Isaak. "I know, my friend. But do you truly know that?" He pulled up a chair and sat directly in front of Isaak, his voice low but steady. "I understand it was an accident, but the queen doesn't care. She wants you to be guilty."

With a grim expression, Aleksi placed the burning rod on Isaak's chest, its heat searing through the fabric of his clothes. "Even then, I still must follow orders," Aleksi continued, his voice laced with a hint of regret. "And you will confess to me—of all your crimes."

The room grew colder as Aleksi pressed on, using increasingly painful methods to extract a confession. Isaak's body tensed with each new torment, the pain blurring his thoughts, as he struggled to make sense of the dark spiral, he was now caught in.

Isaak's body was battered, each blow pushing him further into despair, but even in those fleeting moments of respite between tortures, he clung to whatever semblance of hope remained. He whispered jokes to himself, each one a desperate attempt to keep his morale intact, a fragile defense against the pain. Yet those moments were always ripped away too soon, as Aleksi resumed his cruel interrogation.

With a cruel sneer, Aleksi's fist collided with Isaak's face again. "Who else did you steal from, jester?" The question came with another punch, each one harder than the last, his knuckles bruising further with every blow. Isaak winced, his vision swimming, but he refused to let the man break his spirit completely. Despite the pain, he clung to his fleeting memories of laughter, and the tiny scraps of joy that once filled his life.

Aleksi leaned in closer, his voice cold and demanding. "Tell me, boy, so we may make this shorter than it needs to be." Isaak, battered and broken, could feel his resolve weakening with each blow, each question. Time had lost all meaning—hours blended into days, days into weeks. Every moment felt like an eternity, and his body screamed in protest with each painful movement.

His voice barely a whisper, Isaak gave in to the relentless pressure, the words slipping out of him. "I have also stolen from nobles... but I always gave it to the poor." His confession was laced with exhaustion, each syllable a painful release as he succumbed to the weight of his own guilt and the brutal interrogation. The beatings had slowed, but his spirit was nearly gone.

Aleksi's voice grew softer, colder, as he leaned in, his words a cruel whisper. "Was the old jester the only man you have killed?"

Isaak barely had time to brace himself before Aleksi twisted and snapped his right pinky finger. A howl of pain erupted from Isaak's throat, his body shaking uncontrollably as the pain coursed through him. Tears streamed down his face, but his voice cracked as he responded, broken both physically and emotionally. "Yes... but also no."

Aleksi's lips curled into a twisted grin. "Oh, do tell, jester. Do. Tell."

With those words, Aleksi began to break each of Isaak's fingers, one by one, the crack of bone accompanying the rising agony. With every finger shattered, Isaak's resolve crumbled more, and the truth spilled out, forced from him like blood from a wound. "The others were but brigands... evil doers and enemies of the kingdom." His breath hitched between sobs, each confession a painful surrender.

Isaak, trembling and writhing in agony, forced the words through gritted teeth. "They are people I've killed... but I do not consider them men, for they acted like monsters. For them, I shed no tears." He gasped, his body convulsing with pain. "But the old jester... he is a death I regret. For him, I should be punished."

Aleksi regarded him with a solemn expression, his own turmoil hidden beneath a mask of duty. He gave a small, almost imperceptible nod before raising his fist. "Rest now, jester," he muttered under his breath, his voice heavy with regret.

With one swift, deliberate motion, Aleksi struck Isaak across the temple, knocking him unconscious. The room fell silent save for Isaak's labored breathing as his limp body slumped in the chair.

The heavy wooden doors of the dungeon burst open, slamming against the walls. The King strode in, his regal presence radiating fury, followed by Isaak's friends. "What is the meaning of this? What have you done to my Jester?" he bellowed, his eyes locking onto Isaak's battered and bloodied form.

Rasia's gasp filled the room as her gaze fell on Isaak, unconscious and slumped in his chair. Without hesitation, she rushed to his side, cradling him in her arms. "Oh no, my... my love," she whimpered, her voice breaking. Tears streamed down her face as she gently laid him down on the cold stone floor, her fingers brushing the blood matted in his hair. "What happened to you?"

Her grief quickly turned to rage. She spun around and lunged at Aleksi, knocking him to the ground. "You monster!" she screamed, raining blows upon him with all her strength. "How dare you hurt him!"

Aleksi made no attempt to defend himself, his face grim as he absorbed her fury. The King, watching with a mixture of anger and sorrow, allowed her retaliation to continue for a few moments before stepping in. "Stop, Rasia," he said firmly, his voice tempered with authority. "He's had enough."

Breathing heavily, Rasia relented, her hands trembling as she was pulled back by one of Isaak's friends. Her eyes burned with hatred as she glared at Aleksi, who now struggled to his feet. "I'm sorry," Aleksi said quietly, his voice laced with regret. "I was under orders... from the Queen."

The room fell into an uneasy silence, the weight of betrayal thick in the air. The King's jaw tightened; his hands clenched into fists. "Under her orders?" he repeated, his voice cold as steel. "This will not go unanswered."

Rasia knelt back down beside Isaak, brushing his hair gently. "Hold on, my love," she whispered. "We'll get you out of here."

The King's face turned crimson with fury, his voice booming through the dungeon. "What did you just say?" he demanded, his tone trembling with anger. Aleksi, his head bowed in shame, repeated, "The Queen ordered the jester's hanging tomorrow. I'm sorry, Your Majesty."

Rasia's eyes widened in shock, her rage boiling over. Without hesitation, she stepped forward and struck

Aleksi with such force that he crumpled to the ground, unconscious. "How dare you follow such orders!" she screamed, her voice echoing in the cold chamber.

The King placed a calming hand on her shoulder. "Enough, Rasia. We'll deal with this." His tone was steady, but the fire in his eyes betrayed his fury. He turned to Isaak's friends. "Take him to the royal physician and ensure he's cared for immediately."

Together, the King and Rasia stormed through the palace halls, their footsteps reverberating with purpose. They barged into the Queen's private quarters, where she lounged with an air of indifference.

"How could you, my dear?" the King bellowed, his voice filled with disbelief and betrayal. "How could you go behind my back and do this to poor Isaak?"

Rasia stepped forward, trembling with fury. "That's my love you're trying to hang! How dare you? I should kill you where you stand!" Her voice cracked with emotion as her fists clenched tightly by her sides.

The Queen met their fury with an icy glare, a scoff escaping her lips. "Who cares about some jester dying?" she said dismissively, her voice dripping with disdain. "He's a murderer and a thief. His death is justice."

Rasia's eyes burned with hatred, and even the King seemed stunned into silence for a moment. The tension in the room was thick as the confrontation loomed, emotions teetering on the brink of explosion.

Rasia stepped forward, her voice shaking with anger, but unwavering in its intensity. "I care, you heartless witch!" she shouted, her words slicing through the room like a blade. "And Isaak is no murderer. What happened was an accident!"

Her chest heaved as she glared at the Queen, her emotions raw and exposed. The Queen, taken aback by the outburst, narrowed her eyes but said nothing, her composure momentarily faltering.

The King raised his hand, his expression dark. "Enough, both of you!" he commanded, his voice carrying the authority of his station. "This is not how we resolve matters in this palace."

But Rasia wasn't done. Her voice softened but lost none of its passion. "You don't know him. You don't know the man I love, the man who brings light and joy wherever he goes. He doesn't deserve this cruelty."

The Queen's lips pressed into a thin line; her expression unreadable as the tension in the room grew heavier. The King turned to his wife; his eyes filled with disappointment. "You've gone too far this time," he said, his tone low but firm.

The King sighed deeply, the weight of the situation bearing heavily on him. He knew that stopping the execution would only provoke the Queen further, and her vindictiveness could lead to even darker schemes. His face was etched with frustration and regret. "Rasia," he said quietly, his voice heavy with defeat, "there's nothing we can do for Isaak now. The hanging is set for tomorrow."

Rasia turned to him, her eyes blazing with fury and desperation. "How can you say that?" she demanded, her voice trembling. "You're the King! You have the power to stop this!"

He looked at her with sorrowful eyes, shaking his head slowly. "You don't understand. If I intervene now, she'll find another way—something even worse. I can't protect him if I act rashly." His words were barely above a whisper, laden with resignation.

Rasia's fists clenched at her sides, her body trembling with emotion. "Then you're abandoning him to her cruelty?" she whispered, her voice breaking.

The King placed a gentle hand on her shoulder, his expression pained. "Come, Rasia," he said softly. "Go to him. Say your goodbyes while there's still time."

Rasia pulled away from his touch, her breath hitching as tears filled her eyes. Reluctantly, she allowed herself to be guided back toward Isaak, every step feeling like a betrayal to the man she loved.

CHAPTER ELEVEN:
Medicine and tears

Isaak's eyes fluttered open, the dim light of the infirmary casting a pale glow around the room. His body ached, each movement sending jolts of pain through him. As he attempted to shift, the cold, unyielding feel of chains around his wrists reminded him of his grim reality. He was bound to the bed.

Turning his head slowly, his gaze softened at the sight beside him. His mother sat in a chair, her head resting against the edge of the bed. Her face bore the signs of sleepless nights—her cheeks streaked with dried tears; her eyes swollen even in slumber. She clutched one of his hands in her own, the grip firm yet tender, as if holding on to him with all the strength she had left.

A lump formed in Isaak's throat as he took in the sight. The pain of his injuries seemed to fade, replaced by an ache in his heart. "Mama..." he whispered hoarsely, his voice cracking under the weight of emotion. But she didn't stir, her exhaustion keeping her in a restless sleep.

Isaak stared at her, guilt and sorrow swirling within him. He felt the wetness of his own tears tracing down his cheeks as he whispered, "I'm so sorry, Mama." The words felt hollow, as if they could never undo the anguish he had caused. Isaak's eyes roamed the unfamiliar room, taking in the sterile walls and the faint medicinal scent that lingered in the air. The infirmary was quiet, save for the soft hum of the night and the occasional creak of a floorboard. He winced as the chains binding him clinked with his slightest movement, each motion sending a sharp reminder of his injuries coursing through him.

He turned his head toward his mother, her face etched with weariness even in sleep. Isaak squeezed her hand tightly, as though trying to draw strength from her even as guilt consumed him. "Mama," he murmured, his voice trembling, "I'm so sorry... I killed a man."

His tears fell freely, tracing down his battered face, each drop heavy with regret. The words hung in the air, echoing in the quiet room like a confession to the walls themselves. He wanted her to wake up, to say something—anything—to ease the weight pressing down on his chest. But she remained still, her breathing slow and steady, untouched by his whispered agony.

Isaak closed his eyes briefly, his heart aching as he clung to her hand, seeking solace in her presence even in her silence. The guilt he carried felt unbearable, but in her, he found a faint glimmer of hope, a reminder of what he still had left to protect.

Isaak tightened his grip on his mother's hand, his voice trembling with raw emotion. "Everything hurts,

Mama. My body, my heart, my mind—it all hurts so... so much. It's more than I can bear." His voice cracked, each word heavy with despair. Tears streamed down his face, mixing with the bruises and cuts that adorned him like scars of his torment. "Mama," he whispered, his chest heaving, "would you still love me if you found out that I'm a murderer?"

The silence of the room seemed to deepen; his mother still lost in her restless sleep. Isaak's question lingered in the air, unanswered, until a soft but firm voice broke through. "You are no murderer, little brother."

Isaak's eyes widened as he turned his head toward the door. There stood Wina, her figure illuminated by the dim light filtering through the infirmary window. Her presence was a sudden balm to his anguish, her voice carrying the weight of reassurance he so desperately needed.

She approached him with gentle steps, her expression a mix of determination and concern. Isaak's tears didn't stop, but the faintest glimmer of relief crossed his face as Wina knelt beside him. "You've done things you regret, Isaak," she continued, her tone steady, "but that doesn't make you a murderer. It makes you human."

"Rasia told me everything," Wina said softly, her voice steady yet tinged with sorrow. "You are no murderer, Isaak—it was an accident. She believes in you, and so do I." She sat beside him, her gaze tender as she took in the sight of her wounded brother. "She was here earlier, waiting for you to wake, but she left suddenly. She needed to talk to Joffa and our new brother, Jeremy."

Isaak's tears continued to flow, but Wina's words brought a small comfort, like a warm blanket against a bitter cold. "You know Mama still loves you, regardless of your actions," Wina continued, her own voice beginning to waver. "She knows your heart, your innocence. She even tried to get the queen to reverse her decision, but... she failed."

Her words faltered as tears welled in her eyes, spilling over as she looked at him with unbearable grief. "I'm so sorry, little brother. They... they're going to hang you soon."

Unable to contain her emotions any longer, Wina leaned forward and wrapped her arms around Isaak, holding him close but with the utmost care, mindful of his injuries. Her embrace was gentle but full of desperate love, as if trying to shield him from the cruel fate that awaited him. Isaak closed his eyes, feeling her warmth and the depth of her sorrow, the two siblings clinging to each other in their shared pain.

Wina's shoulders shook as she sobbed quietly, her guilt overwhelming. "I've failed you, brother," she whispered, her voice heavy with regret. "I'm your older sister, and I couldn't protect you. That was my job, and I let you down."

Isaak, despite the pain coursing through his body, managed to lift his hand to hers, squeezing it weakly. His voice was soft yet resolute as he replied, "You have not failed me, sister. What happens to me—it's because of my own actions, not yours."

He looked into her tear-streaked face, his gaze filled with understanding and love. "You've always been there for me, Wina. Always. And even now, you're here. That's what matters. You didn't fail me—you never could."

Wina's sobs grew quieter as she clung to his words, her guilt slowly melting into a bittersweet acceptance. She placed her hand over his, holding it tightly as if her grip alone could keep him tethered to the world. "I love you, little brother," she whispered, her voice trembling but filled with conviction. "No matter what happens, I'll always love you."

Isaak's mother stirred, her eyelids fluttering open to see her son awake. Her heart shattered all over again as her gaze fell on his battered face and fragile frame. Tears poured down her cheeks as she leaned forward, wrapping her arms around him with a soft but desperate embrace.

"My son... my little jester... my Isaak," Yenn whispered through trembling lips, her voice thick with emotion. She held him tightly, as if afraid he might vanish from her arms at any moment. Her tears fell freely onto his shoulder, soaking into his shirt.

"Look at you," she said, her voice breaking as her hand gently touched his bruised cheek. "These bruises, this suffering... that brute Aleksi should be the one hanged, not you."

Isaak tried to speak, but Yenn shook her head, her tears intensifying. "I know you are innocent, my son. No one can tell me otherwise, no matter what they say. You are my child, my sweet boy who brought joy to everyone around him. You don't deserve this."

Her sobs grew louder as she clutched him closer, her maternal instincts screaming to shield him from the cruel world that sought to take him away. "I wish I could save you, Isaak. I would give anything... anything to trade places with you. But I... I can't," she cried, her voice breaking completely as she succumbed to the helplessness of the moment.

Yenn's grip tightened as fresh waves of anguish consumed her. "I should be the one who dies, not my child!" she cried out, her voice heavy with despair. Her arms encircled Isaak protectively, trembling with the weight of her grief. "First my husband, now my baby boy... why has God forsaken me?"

Her tears fell like rain, staining Isaak's tattered shirt, each droplet a testament to her broken heart. Isaak, despite his own pain, gently lifted his hand to her face, his chains clinking softly. With trembling fingers, he wiped away her tears, his touch as light as a whisper.

A small, wistful smile tugged at the corner of his lips as he remembered something—something that once brought his mother joy. In a voice cracked from exhaustion but laced with determination, Isaak recited a joke, a simple quip he and his father had crafted together during one of their rare moments of peace.

"Hey, Mama," he began softly, his voice barely above a whisper. "Why did the jester refuse to play cards with the king?"

Yenn paused, her sobs quieting slightly as she instinctively responded, "Why?"

Isaak mustered the faintest grin. "Because he was tired of dealing with royal flushes!"

The familiar punchline, laden with bittersweet memories, momentarily lifted the gloom. Yenn let out a shaky laugh, her tears mingling with a fragile smile. She clutched her son's hand tightly, cherishing the small piece of light he managed to bring even in the darkest of moments. Isaak closed his eyes, the sound of her laughter—though brief—a balm to his wounded soul.

Isaak's mind drifted back to a simpler time, a memory from his eighteenth birthday. He had been diligently working on his comedy set when he had turned to his father with a request, "Papa, can you help me with a joke?"

Gregori, his father, had paused from his work and grinned. "Sure, boy, but only if you help me feed the cows first."

Without hesitation, Isaak had followed him to the barn, and together they had tended to the animals. While tossing hay and filling troughs, the two brainstormed punchlines. Most of them fell flat, earning only groans or half-hearted chuckles. But then Gregori, his eyes sparkling with mischief, turned to Isaak and asked, "Son, do you know why the chicken crossed the road?"

Isaak tilted his head, genuinely curious. "No...why would a chicken cross a road?"

Gregori burst into laughter before delivering the punchline with exaggerated enthusiasm: "To get to the other side of the road, boy!"

At first, Isaak had tried to stifle his reaction, shaking his head at the absurd simplicity. But soon, he found himself laughing uncontrollably, not at the joke itself but at the sheer joy his father radiated in that moment.

Back in the infirmary, Isaak replayed that memory and shared the joke aloud. "Mama," he began weakly, his voice hoarse but determined, "do you know why the chicken crossed the road?"

Yenn, despite her grief, managed a faint smile, indulging her son. "No, my little jester. Why?"

"To get to the other side of the road, Mama."

Yenn chuckled softly, tears still glistening in her eyes. The joke wasn't particularly funny, but it was drenched in nostalgia, a slice of happiness pulled from their shared past. "Isaak," she said, her voice trembling with affection, "I'm going to miss your jokes."

Isaak smiled faintly, holding onto the bittersweet moment as tightly as he could, cherishing the warmth of his mother's fleeting laughter.

The door creaked open, and a figure stepped into the infirmary wearing the haunting visage of a plague mask. Its dark, hollow eyes and elongated beak cast an eerie shadow across the room. Yenn gasped audibly, instinctively tightening her hold on Isaak, while Wina stepped back, her hand reflexively reaching for something to defend herself with.

Before anyone could speak, the figure quickly raised his hands in apology. With a hurried motion, he removed the mask, revealing a young, slightly flustered doctor. "Oh dear, I'm so sorry! I didn't mean to scare you all," he said, his voice filled with genuine remorse.

The room fell silent for a moment before Yenn cautiously asked, "Then why...why the mask?"

The doctor chuckled nervously, rubbing the back of his neck. "Ah, well, it's not what it looks like. No one here has the plague, I assure you," he explained, holding up the mask as if to offer proof of its harmlessness. "I just came from an autopsy, and the smell of the body was... quite overwhelming. The mask helps with that, you see."

Wina lowered her guard, her initial fear giving way to irritation. "You could've warned us before barging in looking like death itself," she muttered, crossing her arms.

The doctor bowed his head apologetically. "You're absolutely right. I'll remember that for next time." He turned his attention to Isaak, his expression softening as he approached the bed. "Now then, let's see about our patient, shall we?"

The tension in the room eased as the doctor began his work, though the unsettling image of the mask lingered in everyone's minds. Isaak, despite his pain, managed a weak chuckle. "Next time, Doc," he murmured, "just wear perfume."

The doctor grinned sheepishly. "Noted, my jester."

The doctor adjusted his coat, his demeanor shifting to one of professional calm. He cleared his throat before speaking. "I am the resident physician here at the royal palace," he began with a faint chuckle, "and I bring both good news and bad news."

Isaak, weary and worn but always one to appreciate humor, managed a faint smile. "Alright, Doc," he rasped, "hit me with the good news first."

The doctor leaned closer; his voice warm with reassurance. "The good news is that you don't have any infections. Your wounds are clean, and your body is responding well. Under normal circumstances, you'd heal quite nicely."

Isaak's smile widened slightly, but it quickly faltered as he asked, "And the bad news?"

The doctor hesitated for a moment, then offered a self-deprecating chuckle. "Well, the bad news is that we may never get to see that recovery," he said with a grim twist of humor. "Given you're due to be hanged in just a few hours."

The room fell silent, and Isaak blinked at the bluntness of the statement. The doctor immediately raised his hands in apology. "Ah, forgive me for my... gallows humor," he added quickly, his tone genuinely contrite.

Isaak, against all odds, let out a weak laugh. "Gallows humor, huh? That's rich, Doc. Guess I can't fault you for sticking to the theme."

The doctor smiled faintly, bowing his head. "Sometimes humor is the only medicine we have, even in moments like these," he said softly. Wina, standing nearby, glared at the doctor but said nothing, while Yenn simply clung to Isaak, her tears dampening his shoulder.

"Well, Doc," Isaak whispered, "let's hope you've got something stronger than jokes to save me."

The doctor adjusted his spectacles, his voice softening with a touch of optimism. "Well, there is some additional good news," he said, his gaze shifting to Yenn. "We've identified what was ailing your mother. She had a minor infection, but nothing serious. A few cups of herbal tea, some hearty soup, and plenty of rest will do the trick. Of course," he added, reaching into his satchel, "it has to be a specific herb, one that I happen to have on hand."

Yenn looked up, her tear-streaked face lighting up with relief. "Thank you, Doctor," she murmured, clutching Isaak's hand more tightly.

Isaak smiled faintly. "That's a load off my mind," he said. "And the bad news?"

The doctor's expression turned grim, though his tone retained its peculiar levity. "Well, Isaak, the bad news is that none of my remedies can cure what's coming for you." He paused, then added with macabre humor, "I'm afraid no tea, soup, or herbs can heal a snapped neck from the noose."

Isaak blinked, caught off guard for a moment before a weak chuckle escaped him. "Dark, Doc. Real dark," he said, shaking his head.

"I do apologize," the doctor replied with a small bow, his voice sincere. "I often find that humor, however bleak, can lighten heavy hearts."

Isaak laughed again, the sound bittersweet. "Well, at least you're consistent," he said, his tone tinged with appreciation. "And honestly, knowing my mother's going to be okay... that's enough for me."

Yenn's grip on Isaak's hand tightened, her tears flowing anew, but this time there was a glimmer of hope in her eyes. Wina, standing nearby, let out a huff but managed to smile, grateful for any sliver of good news amidst the sorrow.

Isaak looked up at the doctor, his voice soft. "So, Doc, what else can you tell me?"

The doctor shook his head slightly, a small smile tugging at his lips. "Unfortunately, nothing else that's helpful. You're already aware of the situation, and there's not much I can offer beyond what we've discussed." He then turned to Yenn, handing her a small cup of tea. "Here, this should help settle your nerves a bit."

Yenn took the tea with trembling hands, nodding in appreciation. As she sipped it, Isaak's eyes shifted back to her, his voice laden with regret. "Mama, I'm sorry for everything I've done. I've brought so much pain to you, to everyone..."

Before he could say more, his mother quickly shushed him, her arms wrapping around him in a tight, comforting embrace. "No, my son, you have nothing to apologize for." She whispered, her voice a soft tremor.

"You're the best thing in my life. Nothing you did could ever make me stop loving you."

Isaak closed his eyes, allowing himself to lean into the warmth of her embrace, her words soothing the turmoil in his heart. The doctor gently helped Isaak drink some tea, his hands steady despite the heavy atmosphere in the room. Isaak barely noticed the warmth of the drink as the weight of his situation settled deeper in his heart. He could feel the tension in the air, and before he could respond, the door suddenly burst open.

Three guards entered: their footsteps heavy on the stone floor. Without a word, they approached Isaak and roughly seized him.

"It's time for your hanging, Jester," one of the guards said, his tone devoid of any empathy.

Isaak felt the sting of resignation flood his chest, and with no strength left to resist, he let them drag him away. His movements were sluggish, his heart pounding with the knowledge that this was the end. He'd done what he could, and now he would pay for it.

Yenn's voice rang out, desperate and filled with heartbreak. "No, you can't take my son!" she cried, her arms reaching out toward Isaak as the guards ignored her, pulling him down the hall.

Isaak cast one final glance toward his mother, knowing this would be the last time he'd see her, his heart breaking for the pain he was causing her.

The guards continued their cold march, dragging him through the palace and out into the open, where a crowd had already gathered. The morning sun hung low in the sky, casting an orange glow over the scene.

From a distance, Isaak heard a familiar voice, and he turned his head slightly to see his sister, Wina, rushing toward the guards.

"I thought my brother wasn't going to be hanged for another few hours!" she yelled, her eyes filled with outrage.

One of the guards looked down at her, a cold expression on his face. "The queen wanted to do it now. No further delays."

Isaak's heart sank even further as he was dragged toward the gallows, the weight of the world pressing on him as the crowd murmured in anticipation.

The moment had arrived. Isaak stood before the gallows, his hands bound tightly, his body numb from the pain and the weight of what was to come. The trapdoor loomed beneath him, an unavoidable fate. As they fastened the noose around his neck, Isaak's gaze swept across the gathered crowd, his eyes locking onto the faces of those he had touched, those whose lives his actions had altered.

He saw the royal family first—the prince, his face red with anger and the weight of unshed tears. Isaak could feel the prince's frustration, the boy who had tried desperately to delay the hanging in any way he could. Isaak knew he had fought for him, and it saddened him to know that his final act would be so painful for his once friend.

Then, his gaze shifted to the king. The king's face was tight with sorrow, and Isaak's heart ached. He knew that the king had been a source of comfort and laughter for him, but now he wouldn't be able to make him laugh ever again. The weight of that knowledge crushed Isaak.

Next, his eyes fell on the princess. She was clutching her rabbit, sobbing uncontrollably. Isaak had become a friend to her, someone who made her laugh, and now she was losing him. His heart broke for her, and he wished he could comfort her in this moment of pain.

And then, there was the queen. Her sadistic smile was unmistakable, but Isaak refused to let her have the satisfaction of his fear. With what little strength he had left, he made a funny face at her, hoping to rob her of the triumph she so desperately sought. For just a moment, her smile faltered, and Isaak took some solace in that.

Among the crowd, Isaak saw a few cutthroats—the men who had been his companions, who had shared in his more questionable acts. They were protesting his hanging, calling out in anger, perhaps feeling the sting of betrayal in the system that had once allowed them to thrive.

He could also see villagers from across the kingdom, some of whom had once looked to him for entertainment, some who had seen him as a symbol of the kingdom's injustices.

They, too, were protesting—some with shouts, others with solemn faces—as Isaak's fate seemed to rip through the hearts of everyone who had ever known him.

The time was now, and Isaak, though his heart was heavy, found the strength to face it with the one thing he still had—his defiance.

CHAPTER TWELVE:
The Hanged Jester

The man in extravagant attire, voice dripping with disdain, sneered, "Hast thou any final words?"

The jester paused, his eyes searching the faces of the crowd as if drawing strength from their presence. He nodded slowly. "Aye," he replied softly, gathering his thoughts, his mind racing for something to say before the end. His eyes swept the crowd, every face a memory, every gaze a final echo. After a long, pregnant silence, he spoke, his voice carrying with gravity and weight.

"What is a jester?" he asked, his usual playful tone replaced by something deeper. "It is a question I've asked myself countless times—through every place I've wandered, with every soul I've met, and in every jest I've made."

He let his words hang in the air, heavy and reflective. The mischievous glint in his eyes faded, replaced by an unusual solemnity, as though the moment had stripped him of his usual bravado. "Every answer is different, depending on who you ask. Some see us as mere fools, others as entertainers, and some as nuisances to be dismissed. But one answer, one truth, has remained clear to me throughout all the years of laughter and pain." He let the words linger, his voice quiet but resolute. "That answer will remain with me always—like a shadow that follows. It is the sum of every face I've seen, every laugh I've shared, every tear I've hidden. It's not just the good moments that shape us, but the bad ones too."

He paused for a moment, taking a deep breath, his heart heavy with all that he had said, all that he had lived.

The man in extravagant attire, unmoved by the jester's words, gave a sharp, cold signal to the executioner. Without a word, the executioner tightened the noose.

The jester's last breath hitched as the rope pulled tight, stealing the air from his lungs. His neck twisted, strained, and snapping with a sickening crack. And as his life slipped away, the question that had haunted him— What is a jester? —hung in the air, unanswered, a lingering riddle to be carried on by those who had known him. As the final moments of Isaak's life hung in the air, the sharp tension of the noose around his neck was suddenly cut. With a sickening jolt, Isaak collapsed to the ground, gasping for breath, his body aching from the strain. His hand instinctively went to his neck, feeling the burn of the rope. As he rose shakily to his feet, he glanced around and saw a sea of shocked faces, and amidst the crowd, the Queen's furious gaze bore into him. She screamed for the guards, her voice full of rage and disbelief.

But before the guards could close in, Joffa was at Isaak's side, swiftly cutting through the remaining ropes that bound him. "Your friend Jeremey is quite the marksman," Joffa said with a grin, his eyes glancing at the gallows where the rope had been severed by a perfectly aimed arrow. Isaak's gaze followed the path of the projectile, a slow smile tugging at his lips as he realized what had just saved his life.

Joffa handed Isaak his hatchet, his expression turning serious. "It's time to fight, Jester. Let's make our escape."

With a grin, Isaak took the weapon, his heart racing with a mix of exhilaration and adrenaline. In a flash, he was at Joffa's side, fighting alongside the cutthroats and villagers who had rallied to his cause. The clash of steel and the shouts of combat filled the air as they took on a dozen royal guards. The King, though troubled by the chaos, could be seen cheering Isaak on from the sidelines, his face a mixture of disbelief and admiration for the courage of the condemned jester. Isaak's laughter echoed across the platform, louder than the clang of swords, as the tide of battle began to turn in their favor.

Furious beyond measure, the Queen snatched a sword from one of the guards and charged at Isaak, her fury blinding her. But her strike went wide, and Isaak dodged effortlessly, his eyes dancing with amusement. Before she could swing again, Rasia charged in like a storm, landing a powerful sucker punch that sent the Queen stumbling backward. The two women went at it, fists flying with a wild ferocity. Rasia landed several solid blows, each one fueled by years of pent-up frustration, but the Queen was no novice. With a sneer, she reached into her sleeve and flung a handful of sand straight into Rasia's eyes, blinding her temporarily.

Isaak, still battling off guard, couldn't resist making light of the chaos. Between swipes of his hatchet and dodges from the guards, he called out to the Queen, his voice full of jest. "What's the matter, Your Majesty? Afraid a little sand will ruin your beauty?" His grin only grew wider when he saw the Queen scowl in his direction, her focus momentarily diverted.

Taking advantage of the distraction, Rasia recovered her vision and landed a swift, well-placed kick to the Queen's stomach, sending her reeling. Isaak laughed loudly, continuing to taunt the Queen, his jokes flying even as he fought off the guards with impressive agility. "You know, I always thought you were a bit full of yourself, but I didn't realize it was because you were stuffed with sand!" The Queen snarled, her anger only escalating, but the moment was just enough for Rasia to press her advantage, and Isaak, with his usual irreverence, kept the distractions coming.

Aleksi entered the fray with a cold smirk, immediately locking eyes with Joffa. "You're no match for me, you overgrown ox," Aleksi taunted, his dagger flashing as he aimed for Joffa's side. The strike, however, had no effect on the giant man, who simply grunted and laughed.

"Ha, that's all you got, Aleksi? One measly stab?" Joffa bellowed, swatting the smaller man's attack aside with ease. In one swift motion, he grabbed Aleksi by the collar and hurled him across the room, sending him crashing into the wall with a loud thud.

Aleksi, barely missing a beat, sprang to his feet, his face twisted in anger. The two men locked in a fierce grapple, each one struggling to overpower the other. Muscles strained as they fought for dominance, hands gripping each other's arms and throats in a desperate attempt to force the other into submission. The room echoed with the sounds of their struggle, the clashing of bodies and grunts of exertion filling the air. Aleksi's lithe frame may have been nimble, but Joffa's sheer strength made him a formidable opponent, and neither was willing to relent.

The battle between the two was far from over, each one determined to prove their superiority.

Isaak, growing weaker under the relentless pressure of the guards, found himself overwhelmed. Just as the situation seemed hopeless, a familiar voice cut through the chaos. "Sister? Jeremey?" Isaak gasped, astonished.

In an instant, Wina and Jeremey appeared, side by side, their movements swift and precise. With expert coordination, they each took down four guards, their weapons flashing as they disabled their foes with lethal efficiency. Wina's swift strikes and Jeremey's sharp precision turned the tide of the battle, and Isaak, revitalized by their timely arrival, regained his footing. Together, they fought through the melee, a force to be reckoned with, cutting down their enemies and pushing back the advancing guards.

The king, utterly fed up with his wife's tyranny and the chaos unfolding, made a sudden decision to join the fray. Gripping his Warhammer with a fierce determination, he waded into the fight, targeting his own guards. The guards, taken aback by their king's unexpected participation, found themselves quickly overwhelmed as the king's powerful blows sent them crashing to the ground, their confusion giving way to defeat.

Meanwhile, the battle between the queen and Rasia escalated with every passing second. Each punch, each kick, and even hair pulls and bites became more brutal, their fight a raw, unrelenting clash of fury. Rasia's relentless determination met the queen's devious tricks, neither willing to give an inch. The tension between them reached its peak, as they tore into each other with every ounce of strength they had left.

The chaos of the battle intensified as more villagers, emboldened by Isaak's defiance, rushed to his aid. The sound of clashing swords and grunts of exertion filled the air, but through it all, Isaak's laughter rang out, cutting through the noise like a sharp knife. His jokes, relentless and teasing, only seemed to irritate the queen further, her fury growing with every punch he threw, every quip he made.

Meanwhile, Isaak and the King stood back-to-back, fighting side by side, each delivering ridiculous jokes to keep the spirits high amidst the chaos. The King's laughter grew louder with each guard he struck down, the sound a booming contrast to the brutal clash around them. With every joke, their bond seemed to strengthen, the absurdity of the situation fueling their camaraderie as they made light of the war raging on around them.

Finally, Isaak collapsed, falling to his knees in agony, unable to continue the fight. The King rushed to his side; his face full of concern as he checked Isaak's wounds. "Stop! Enough of this!" he bellowed. At his command, the fighting ceased abruptly—guards froze in place, and even the villagers halted their attacks.

Aleksi, unable to withstand Joffa's relentless headlock, lost consciousness. Yet, the Queen and Rasia continued their brutal brawl, locked in a frenzy of punches and rage. It wasn't until the King, with a powerful grip, seized the Queen from behind that the battle came to a halt.

"Stop, enough, my love. You've done enough," the King's stern voice cut through the air, shocking the Queen into stillness. He turned her to face the chaos she had caused, his voice hardening with fury. "Look at this mess you've made. This carnage—all because you wanted to hang an innocent jester. For what?" His finger pointed at Isaak, who was gasping for breath, his body wracked with pain from the brutal fight.

"Look at him, my dear... Look at him," the King urged, his voice filled with a mix of sorrow and anger. The Queen turned her gaze to Isaak, and in that moment, a wave of realization washed over her—of all the suffering she had caused. Her eyes welled with tears as she began to cry, her voice broken with apologies.

But the King was unmoved. "An apology isn't enough, my love," he replied coldly. Turning to his guards, he commanded, "Arrest my wife, the Queen. She is to remain in the dungeon for an entire year."

As the guards moved to obey, Isaak, his body still aching, weakly rose to his feet and intervened. "No, Your Majesty... It's okay," he said, his voice steady despite the pain. Isaak turned to the Queen; his gaze steady but forgiving. "I accept your apology, but you are no longer fit to be a queen," he said, his tone firm but not harsh. With a swift motion, he sprayed her with a burst of colorful water, the vibrant stream catching the light. "You need to lighten up, my queen."

For a moment, the Queen stood in stunned silence, her face frozen in disbelief. Then, as the water dripped from her, something inside her cracked. A laugh bubbled up from deep within her, unexpected and genuine. Isaak joined in, his laughter ringing out as the tension that had once gripped them all began to dissolve.

"You're right, Jester," she said between breaths of laughter, her voice softening. "Maybe I do need to lighten up."

But before Isaak could say another word, his mother stormed forward, her face red with fury. Without hesitation, she slapped the Queen across the face. "That's for my son, you bitch!" she spat, her words sharp and full of a mother's wrath.

The king's laughter boomed through the chaos, his deep chuckles filling the air as he finally regained his composure. He glanced at his wife with a rueful smile, offering a sincere apology for the laughter that had just escaped him. "Forgive me, my dear," he said, his voice softening.

The queen stood there, her expression one of regret and resolve. With a heavy heart, she spoke, her voice carrying the weight of her decision. "I hereby abdicate," she declared, her words echoing in the room. "I will no longer be your queen. And to atone for my sins, I shall exile myself."

Her gaze swept over the assembled group, lingering on Isaak, his mother, and the king. "I am sorry," she said, her voice breaking. "Sorry to all of you... and especially to you, my love."

The king nodded somberly, understanding the gravity of her words. "I need to do this, my love," the queen whispered, almost to herself. Without another word, she turned and walked out of the palace, her footsteps fading into the distance. She left the kingdom behind, never to be heard from again.

The King turned to Isaak; his expression filled with remorse. "I'm sorry this all happened, my boy," he said, his voice heavy with regret.

Isaak shook his head, his gaze falling to the ground. "No, my king, I'm sorry," he replied, his voice tinged with guilt. "This was all because of me. I don't deserve any apologies, nor do I deserve to be your jester."

The king let out a hearty laugh, just as he always had, a sound that echoed with warmth and reassurance. "Nonsense, my boy," he said, patting Isaak on the shoulder. "You've done no wrong. What happened was not your fault."

The king then began to recount a short story, one from his youth, before he had ascended to the throne. It was a tale of a similar incident—one that had involved him directly. Isaak listened intently, the weight of his own guilt starting to lift with each word the king spoke.

By the time the story came to an end, Isaak felt a lightness in his chest. The king's words had eased the burden he had carried for so long, and for the first time in a while, he allowed himself to believe that he might not be entirely to blame for everything that had transpired.

"Isaak, my boy," the King began, his tone gentle yet full of hope, "would you still want to be my jester?"

Isaak stood still, lost in thought. The weight of the question hung in the air as he reached down and picked up his cracked mask. He placed it carefully on his face, and with a mischievous smile, he replied, "Well, my king, this should answer your question."

With that, Isaak performed a graceful flip, landing with a flourish, and delivered a quick joke. The King erupted in laughter, the sound warm and genuine, before pulling Isaak into a tight hug. "I'm glad you're okay, my boy," he said, his voice thick with affection.

Isaak's heart lightened as the King cleared his throat, signaling that he was about to make an important announcement.

"I hereby pardon Isaak, the King of Fools, of all his crimes," the King proclaimed, his voice echoing through the room. "And if anyone has a problem with that, you can always take a tour of the dungeon." He finished with a chuckle, a twinkle of amusement in his eyes as the court erupted in laughter.

The tension in the air dissolved, replaced by the sound of joyful relief. Isaak's smile widened, and for the first time in what felt like forever, he felt truly at peace.

Isaak then was hugged from behind by Rasia who then pulled him in for a long kiss.

The two embraced, holding each other tightly as if time itself had paused. "I thought I would have lost you, my love," Rasia whispered, her voice trembling with emotion as she clung to Isaak, not wanting to let go.

Isaak smiled softly, his heart swelling with warmth as he gently replied, "And I thought I'd never see you again, Rasia."

With a swift motion, Isaak drew a single rose from his pocket and knelt before Rasia, his heart in his eyes. "Rasia, ever since the moment I met you, you've occupied my thoughts as the queen of bandits, now a mercenary. Yet, beneath it all, you still have that heart that I love. Will you take this foolish man and keep him by your side forever?"

Rasia giggled, a playful spark in her eyes. "Are you trying to propose?"

Isaak chuckled; his smile wide. "Trying, yes. Succeeding... I'm not sure."

With a soft laugh, Rasia accepted the rose. "Of course, I'd marry you."

The two embraced, their hearts full of joy and relief, and the king, beaming with happiness, joined in the embrace, his hearty laughter ringing through the air. "Oh, you must have the wedding here, in the palace! I insist!"

he exclaimed, his voice warm and genuine. "It would be an honor to witness such a joyous occasion."

Isaak and Rasia laughed together, sharing a moment of pure happiness, before Isaak's mother rushed forward, her face streaked with tears of joy. She pulled her son into another tight embrace, her voice trembling with emotion. "I can't believe it, Isaak. My son, you're okay, and now you're engaged! I'm so proud of you, my dear boy. You've come so far."

Isaak smiled through his own tears, squeezing his mother tightly. "I couldn't have done it without you, Mama. Without all of you," he said, glancing around at Rasia, the king, and the others who had fought for him.

Rasia stood beside Isaak, her hand resting gently on his. "We've all come together, against so many odds," she said, her voice filled with conviction. "And now, we'll face whatever comes next, together."

The king nodded, his smile wide. "Indeed, together. The future is bright for you both, my dear jester and soon-to-be bride." He turned to the rest of the court, raising his voice to draw attention. "Let it be known, the wedding will take place right here in this palace, and all who wish to witness this celebration of love, loyalty, and new beginnings are welcome."

The room buzzed with excitement and congratulations, the weight of the past finally lifting. Isaak and Rasia, surrounded by family and friends, felt the joy of a new chapter beginning—one filled with hope, laughter, and the promise of a future built together. Isaak's mother turned toward the king; her expression filled with gratitude. "I must thank you for taking care of my son. How can I ever repay you?" she asked, her voice sincere.

The king smiled warmly; his eyes filled with genuine kindness. "No need to repay me, my lady," he said. "But there is one thing I do require. Now that my wife is gone, I am in need of someone to care for my children. Would you be willing to act as a nanny for them?"

Isaak's mother, touched by the king's request and the trust he was placing in her, agreed without hesitation. "I would be honored, Your Majesty," she replied, her voice soft with emotion.

The king nodded, a small, appreciative smile playing on his lips. As they walked off together to discuss the details, the conversation between them shifted ever so slightly, a hint of flirtation slipping into their words.

Meanwhile, Isaak turned toward the prince, who gave him a teasing smile. "Isaak, I'm glad you're okay," Prince Walter said with a chuckle. "But I must admit, I'm a bit sad you asked Rasia to marry you instead of me."

Isaak laughed, shaking his head. "Well, my prince, you'll have to settle for being my friend instead," he teased, his tone light and playful.

Before Walter could respond, the princess rushed into the room, her face brightening as soon as she saw Isaak. Without hesitation, she threw her arms around him in a tight hug, her relief palpable. "I'm so glad you're okay, Isaak!" she exclaimed, her voice filled with warmth and affection.

Isaak smiled, returning her hug. "Thank you, Princess. It's good to be back," he replied, feeling the bond of family and friendship growing stronger with every passing moment.

CHAPTER THIRTEEN:
Epilogue

A month had passed, and the kingdom had slowly returned to a sense of normalcy. Isaak's performances continued to bring joy and laughter to the people, especially the king, who watched with pride as Isaak's wit and humor filled the halls of the royal palace. But today was different. Today was the day of his wedding.

Isaak stood before the mirror in his room, his heart racing with nervous anticipation. He stared at his reflection, the weight of the moment settling in. "I finally see what you both see, Mama... Rasia... I finally see," he whispered to himself, his voice tinged with a mix of gratitude and realization.

He was dressed in a regal-looking suit, one that he wasn't entirely comfortable in. The fine fabric and elaborate design felt too stiff compared to the freedom of his jester's outfit, which had always been his preferred attire. But today, he was stepping into a new chapter of his life, and he had to honor the occasion.

As Isaak adjusted his collar, his eyes were drawn to the painting of his father, displayed prominently on his desk. A soft, melancholic smile crossed his face as he gazed at the image. "I wish you were here, Papa," he murmured, his voice thick with emotion.

He leaned over, pressing a gentle kiss to the painting's frame, his fingers lingering on the glass for a moment longer. After a brief pause, Isaak carefully returned the painting to its place, feeling a mixture of sorrow and pride. Though his father was no longer by his side, Isaak could feel his presence, guiding him in every step he took toward his future.

Isaak left his room, a smile tugging at the corners of his mouth as he stepped into the hallway. There, in the corner of the corridor, he saw his pet pig, a cheerful little creature, wearing a dapper little hat that sat crookedly on atop its head. The pig was oinking happily, waddling around in circles as it played with Zigbar, the rabbit, who hopped around in joyful abandon.

Isaak couldn't help but laugh at the sight of his two beloved animals, their playful antics a welcome distraction from the weight of the day. "Hello, you two," he greeted warmly, crouching down to stroke both of them, his heart lifting at their innocent joy. They had been with him through so much, a constant source of comfort and amusement.

Zigbar nudged his hand with his nose, and the pig snorted affectionately, both animals seemingly content in each other's company. Isaak chuckled softly, feeling the familiar bond with his furry companions, their carefree nature a reminder of the simple joys that still remained, even in the most tumultuous of times.

Isaak continued down the hallway, his footsteps echoing softly in the quiet palace. As he turned a corner, he spotted Joffa, who had just finished packing his belongings. Isaak paused, a curious look crossing his face. "Joffa, you are going somewhere?" he asked, his voice filled with a mixture of surprise and concern.

Joffa smiled warmly, a bittersweet expression crossing his features as he stepped forward and enveloped Isaak in a heartfelt hug. "I'm sorry, my friend," Joffa said, his voice thick with emotion. "As much as I wish I could stay and witness your wedding, I must return home. My wife and children need me. I've received word that they're in need of my help."

Isaak felt a pang in his chest at the thought of parting with his loyal friend, but he understood. With a tearful smile, he pulled back from the embrace. "I'll miss you, Joffa," he said, his voice cracking slightly. "But I understand. Family always comes first."

The two men exchanged a final, heartfelt look, their bond stronger than words could express. Joffa clapped Isaak on the shoulder one last time before turning to leave, his figure growing smaller as he made his way out of the palace.

Isaak, though saddened, continued on his way, wiping a stray tear from his cheek. He walked through the corridors, each step taking him closer to the next chapter of his life. Finally, he reached the grand doors of the palace church, the soft hum of the gathered crowd inside filling the air. With a deep breath, he stepped forward, ready to face the day that would forever change his life.

Isaak entered the grand hall of the palace church, his eyes scanning the crowd of familiar faces. Among the guests were a few villagers who had come to witness this special day, and Old Henry, along with his friends, stood in the corner, smiling warmly at him. Isaak made his way to the front, taking his place in front of the king, who would be officiating the ceremony.

The king leaned in close, whispering congratulations to Isaak, his voice filled with a genuine fondness. Isaak gave a small, grateful smile, his heart swelling with appreciation for the support of his king and friend.

The room fell silent as the music began to play. An elderly woman sat at the organ, her fingers gracefully dancing across the keys, filling the church with a soft, melodic tune. As the music swelled, the doors at the far end of the room opened, and in walked Rasia, her stride steady and strong. However, instead of a traditional wedding gown, she wore regal battle attire, her armor glinting in the light, and her expression as fierce as ever.

Isaak couldn't help but chuckle, his eyes widening with surprise and amusement as she approached. Rasia caught his gaze and, with a playful whisper, leaned in close to him. "I didn't feel comfortable in a dress," she said, her voice soft but filled with mischief.

Isaak stifled his laughter, his eyes twinkling with amusement as the two shared a brief moment of quiet joy amidst the formality of the occasion.

As the king stood before Isaak and Rasia, the gathered guests, and the royal court, he cleared his throat and spoke with the authority and warmth that came naturally to him. His voice echoed in the grand church, but there was a tenderness in it that could not be mistaken.

"Today, we stand in the presence of something far greater than a union of two individuals. Today, we witness the joining of two hearts, two souls, bound not just by love but by strength, courage, and a shared understanding of the world they inhabit.

Isaak, the King of Fools, the jester who has made us laugh, made us think, and reminded us that even in our darkest moments, there is light to be found in humor. You have shown that a man's worth is not defined by his station, but by his heart and his actions. You have been a loyal companion, a friend, and a voice of truth in a world that often forgets the value of joy. And today, you are no longer just the jester, but a man who has earned his place, not just by the crown, but by the love you've found with Rasia.

And Rasia... the warrior, the mercenary, the woman of unyielding strength and fierce loyalty. You wear your armor like a shield to the world, but it is your heart that has been your truest weapon. You are a woman of great conviction, and yet, through all the battles you have fought, it is love that has brought you here today. Not just a love for Isaak, but a love for life itself, for the people you protect, and for the man you choose to stand beside. You have chosen him not for his title, but for the man he is — a man who brings out the best in you and in those around him.

Together, you form a bond that transcends the simple union of marriage. You both challenge one another, lift each other up, and offer each other the kind of love that will weather every storm, no matter how fierce. As the King, I have witnessed many unions, but none as unique and as beautiful as this one.

So, Isaak and Rasia, as you stand here before me, know that this is not merely the joining of two people, but the joining of two worlds. May you always find strength in each other, laughter in every moment, and love in every trial. You are now partners, not just in this life, but in whatever comes after. And I have no doubt that the joy and laughter you bring to this world will continue to echo through the halls of this kingdom for many years to come.

It is my greatest honor to pronounce you not just husband and wife, but champions of one another's hearts.

May your marriage be filled with the same adventure, laughter, and love that you have shown us all.

By the power vested in me, I now declare you united in matrimony. May your journey together be as extraordinary as the love that has brought you here today."

With a final nod of approval, the king stepped back, smiling warmly at the couple before him. The guests erupted into applause, and Isaak and Rasia shared a brief, tender glance, knowing that their future had just begun.

Isaak cleared his throat, a playful twinkle in his eyes as he looked at Rasia. "Before I seal this wondrous day with a kiss that will surely go down in history, I'd like to say a few words," he said, his voice filled with both jest and sincerity.

Rasia's smile softened as she stood by him, ready to hear the words of the man she had come to love beyond measure. Isaak took a deep breath, gathering his thoughts as he turned to address the gathered crowd.

"Thank you, Your Majesty, for those gracious words. And thank you all, for being here with us today, to witness a moment that's difficult to capture in words. But I'll try my best," Isaak began, his voice steady and filled with emotion.

"I've lived many lives, each one more peculiar than the last. I've been the fool, the jester, the one who made you laugh when life seemed far too serious. I've worn a mask and told jokes when all I had to offer was a smile. I've made mistakes—some I've learned from, others I've had to pay for. But as I stand here today, I realize that all of it—the laughter, the tears, the foolishness—has brought me to this very moment. To this day, with all of you. And most importantly, with you, Rasia."

He turned to face her, his eyes softening with every word. "Rasia, my love, you've taught me what it truly means to fight for what's worth fighting for. You've shown me that love isn't something soft and fragile, but a force—a battle that we fight side by side. You've been my strength when I had none, my courage when I doubted myself. I don't deserve you, and yet, by some miracle, you chose me. And for that, I will spend every day of my life proving to you just how much I love you."

The crowd fell silent, hanging on to every word as Isaak's voice grew more earnest. "The world may call me the King of Fools, but you, Rasia—you see me. You see past the jokes, past the mask, past the foolishness—and you love me all the same. And that, my love, is something I will never take for granted. I don't know what I did to deserve such love, but I will spend every day trying to be the man worthy of it."

Isaak reached out, taking her hands in his. "From this day on, I promise you, Rasia, I will never stop laughing with you. I will never stop fighting for you. And I will never stop loving you. Because you, Rasia, are not just my heart or my reason... you are my forever. You're my everything."

He turned to face the crowd once more, his heart full. "To the future, my love... and to us."

With that, Isaak stepped closer to Rasia, his eyes shining with love and laughter as he finally sealed his vows with a kiss, one that would last a lifetime.

The crowd erupted into cheers, their applause filling the air as the final kiss sealed Isaak and Rasia's vows. The cheers echoed through the grand hall, marking the end of this chapter in the jester's life. But while this was the closing of one story, it was far from the end of his journey. Isaak's life, though full of joy and laughter, was never one to be defined by ease. Greater challenges awaited him on the horizon, challenges that would test his resolve and his heart. But one thing was certain: no matter what lay ahead, Isaak would face it all with the same unshakable smile and unwavering spirit that had defined him from the start.

And so, for now, we say goodbye to this tale of love, drama, and laughter. But rest assured, the story of Isaak the Jester is far from over. Until next time, remember that laughter is always the best way to face whatever comes your way.

This... is the end—for now.